CONQUEROR

DEFIER SERIES BOOK THREE

MANDY FENDER

Editor: Elizabeth Miller

Book Cover Design: Mandy Fender

ISBN-13: 978-0-9985657-3-6

Stouthearted Publishing

But the one
who stands
firm to the end
will be saved.

Matthew 24:13

Chapter 1

One month, two days, and eighteen hours…

… without Sky.

The earth spun too fast. Lennox slept too little. But time moved forward as if everything was normal.

As if living in the midst of Armageddon could ever be considered "normal."

At the Sparrow base of operations, in a canvas tent located discretely along the edge of nowhere and hidden behind Texas pines, Lennox stood with her peers, awaiting orders. She curled her toes against the soles of her black, military-grade boots as a hologram image of the Sparrows' founder, Eli, popped up in the middle of their makeshift strategy room. Eli's long and scraggly beard was stark white against his dark, wrinkled skin. His kind brown eyes still held light in them.

"Listen up." The image flickered as the audio distorted his voice. "We have just received word from our outriders that over fifty Defiers, and even a few of our own hostage Sparrows, are being held at a Regime stronghold two hundred miles out from your location. It's imperative that we dispatch a team immediately. It won't be an easy mission, but easy is not what we signed up for. Sparrows, I am praying for your safety. Go with God." Eli fizzled into nothing and the light from the hologram returned to its portal.

Lennox popped her thumbs between her other fingers. Immersing herself in the field was all she could do now to keep some semblance of clear-headedness. Purpose occupied her thoughts instead of dwelling on Sky and everyone else she lost.

Captain Easton stood in the center of the group. All eyes focused on her. As usual, her dark hair was wrapped in a bun at the base of her neck and a gray patrol cap sat neatly on her head. "At oh-five hundred, a Sparrow stealth plane will arrive to take the designated team to the drop-point forty miles out. The pilots can't get you any closer than that. From there you'll advance." Her eyes darted between the soldiers' faces before her. "If I call your name, head straight for the artillery tent and prepare yourself for combat." She glanced down at her tech screen and rattled off names, starting with the lead paratroopers. "Edwards, Hershall, Jones, Pearson...."

As her fellows stepped forward, Lennox scrunched her toes harder in her boots, hoping for her name to be called as a combat medic.

"L. Winters."

Finally. Lennox stepped to the front, nodded to her Captain, and then headed to check her weapons, as ordered.

"Sparrow Winters."

Lennox stopped and faced Captain Easton.

"With Medic Larson out of commission, you'll be Lead Medic."

Lennox's heart thudded in her chest. "Yes ma'am."

In the artillery tent, over twenty highly trained Sparrows strapped ammo to their chests and gathered weapons. Lennox walked to a table full of medical supplies and placed the essentials in her medic bag—trauma bandages and shears, IV fluids, tubing, tourniquets, and a surgical Cricothyrotomy kit. Behind her, someone poked her in the ribs. She jumped and sucked in a breath.

"Sorry, I didn't mean to scare you." Ace's southern twang almost brought her pulse back down to normal.

"You didn't scare me, just caught me off-guard a bit." She smiled and shot a quick glance up at him.

He stood beside her, giving his gear a once-over and then watched her as she steadily zipped up her bag and strapped it to her back. When she headed to the weapons table to pick up her Stryker and sidearm, Ace followed.

He shook his head with each step. "After all they've done, we still don't kill them." He peered through her, like she wasn't even there while he loaded his weapon.

Loading her own gun with the mag full of tiny glowing blue bullets on one side and lethal ammunition on the other, Lennox tried to think of a response that had meaning. She understood his feelings, but pushed herself to say what she knew was truer than what they felt was deserved. "If Jesus can forgive, we can at least try, right?" It seemed silly now to try to forgive, or even explain it, but wasn't that what Jesus would do? Of course He would, though sometimes she did not understand why.

Ace licked his lips. Sweat still beaded on his perfectly smooth skin. "Humph. I guess you're right. I'm just not at that point. I want them all dead, every last one of them." His voice's lack of fluctuation stung and he refused to look at Lennox. His stone-cold face stared at the non-lethal ammunition as if he could change its effectiveness by avoiding her eyes.

A frosty chill ran down Lennox's spine. That's what she really wanted, too, in her flesh. She wanted them all dead for what they had done, for what they turned the world into. The Regime would kill every last Defier and Sparrow if the opportunity presented itself.

Lennox's moral compass spun. If they turned into bloodthirsty, vengeful soldiers, repaying evil with evil, how were they any different than the Regime? *We wouldn't be.* Lennox battled her thoughts. How much of this war had consumed her soul?

Ace turned to her. "Are you scared?"

"Oh, all the time and I have to fight it with every ounce of strength I've got because I *know* how this all ends." Lennox shook her head. "In the end, we win." She fought against her internal fear with every breath. "I will not live in fear of the darkness in this world. I know too much about the light." She stared straight into Ace's deep brown eyes and asked, "Are you scared?"

He answered with a wordless admission.

She placed a gentle hand over his, stopping him from fidgeting with his gear. "Ace, fear only has as much power as we give it. We just have to remember that."

His eyes met hers as he snapped an adaptor blade to his uniform. "I know," he said barely above a whisper.

She curved her lips upward, trying to give him some sort of comfort, and then removed her hand. Even though she struggled with it herself, she spoke the unrelenting truth—the truth that stuck with her and would not let her go. "The beautiful thing is that, even in the darkest of times, there is Jesus. He is light. He is hope." She bit her bottom lip as she took in her own words. She could not let this war defeat her.

Ace forced a half-hearted smile onto his face and nodded as he continued to fiddle with his supplies.

In her peripheral vision, her brother entered the tent. "I'll be right back." She patted Ace's shoulder on the way to Oliver. "Oliver, what are doing here? I thought you had orders to stay put until—"

Oliver stuck up a hand to stop her. "I don't have much time before you have to leave." He looked down at his watch and chewed the inside of his cheek. "You have just a few minutes."

"What is it?" Lennox furrowed her brows.

"The outriders sent me a private message. This isn't an ordinary rescue." Oliver's hazel eyes softened and he took a breath. "It's Sky. We think he's alive."

Lennox nearly lost her balance and grabbed hold of her brother's arm as tears welled.

Oliver placed a hand over hers. "*If* it is him and we can get him, Eli wants to bring him home."

Lennox worried for the safety of her comrades. "What about the Prowler Venom in his veins? How will anyone get close enough to—?"

"The outriders are already in place, just waiting on the rest of the Sparrows to arrive before they enter the stronghold. Their sole purpose is to find him and to bring him home."

A single teardrop ran down her cheek as she wrapped her brother in a hug. "Oh, thank God!"

Oliver returned her hug just as tight before he released her slowly, holding his hands on her shoulders. "We're going to get him back, Len. *We're going to get him back.*"

A commotion outside stole both of their attention.

"Sounds like your ride's here." Oliver brought her close again. "Be safe."

After her brother let her go, Lennox tucked her gear in place and tugged against the straps of her pack. "I will."

Leaving Oliver behind, Lennox met back up with Ace, who was already on the plane.

Her long-awaited prayers were finally going to be answered. Sky was coming home.

Chapter 2

Lennox sat on a tree limb with binoculars, scoping enemy territory for another rescue mission. She watched as men in black uniforms paraded around with guns, coaxing innocents—Defiers—into a line. To the right, a pair of men stood guard in a tower that sat two stories high. An electric fence surrounded the stronghold.

Lennox transitioned her sights back to the Defiers. Some of the larger men puffed out their chests and stubbornly moved slower than the rest as if to challenge the Regime soldiers' authority. Their acts of rebellion were met with butts of rifles to their guts. A lump formed in her throat and the heaviness of the scene made her impatient. She dug her nails deep into her palms, anxious for confrontation.

Come on! Her nerves ticked away the time. Seconds felt like minutes... too long... too slow. She was ready to break in and relieve the enemy of their prisoners, but she had to wait for the other Sparrow teams to survey their zones just as she was clearing hers.

The hour for fighting back in a bigger way was now. The news of the Regime epicenter crumbling down had started a massive rebellion behind the chain-link, electrified fences. One that could make the Regime shrink back like the cowards they were. The embers within Defier hearts ignited flames of faith and hope that shook Regime walls. The Regime could not kill believers fast enough. Many prisoners converted to Christianity from the witness of another, even a few guards did, too. Defiers multiplied with every account of truth spoken, and were now a bigger force to be reckoned with, doing just as the scripture had said, overcoming by the Blood of the Lamb and the word of their testimony. Ahab's day was coming, and the thought made Lennox smile. The enemy's reign was short.

Lennox lowered her binoculars. Ace stood at

the base of the tree, waiting for word from her on their next move. The two made a good surveillance team. Lennox, the scout, Ace, the muscle. She looked down at her impatient comrade.

His dark brows drew together, crinkling his onyx skin as he peered up at her. "What do you see up there?" His southern roots accentuated the vowels and drew out every word. He shifted his weight and crossed his arms, appearing as impatient as Lennox felt. They wanted to find out the truth about Sky. Was he dead? Alive? No one *really* knew. "Can we move in yet?"

"Just a sec." Lennox held the advanced binoculars up to her eyes again. "They're on the move." She counted the Regime soldiers.

Was this how the Israelite spies felt counting the sons of Anak? The Regime was as a giant with their oversized fire-wielding weapons, and the Defiers as grasshoppers, with the only visible weapon being their frail, malnourished bodies. No matter. Faith was the invisible weapon that steadily brought the Regime down one valiant act at a time. God was still on their side. He proved it on several missions and she trusted He would again.

She pressed the binoculars tighter and gasped. There he was! She knew Sky's broad shoulders, six-foot tall frame, and messy dark hair anywhere. He turned, revealing his profile. Lennox shifted on the branch, stretching her neck out farther to get the closest look of him she could. His cheekbones carved a hard line to his lips. His tanned skin was visibly bruised. His walk was all too familiar—one of confidence and balance. He moved freely about the prisoners, working alongside the other Regime soldiers, but he was alive. Lennox allowed her heart to feel what she had tucked deep away for so long... *hope*.

"Sky..." she whispered. His movements, his demeanor, everything about him was Sky, but....

Her mind had played tricks on her before. She blinked hard twice and looked again. She'd watched him walk the tunnels at Sparrow City, seen him in an enemy Humvee, in a safe zone, protecting Defier kids, and in her dreams. He was always in her dreams. She refused to believe he was gone and now she was close to finding out for certain that he lived.

He's alive.

That feeling stayed in her gut and would not

leave.

Ace cleared his throat. "Lennox?"

Lennox snapped herself back to attention, gripping the binoculars with white knuckles. Sky morphed into a being who was no longer Sky. She had imagined him once again—all in her head. The hope in Lennox's heart dissipated as the image of her lost best friend faded into a man who was clearly a Regime officer. *Pull yourself together, Lennox.* Finally, looking down at her partner, she said, "Looks like there's more than a dozen standing guard, probably more throughout the camp, too."

Ace nodded, sweat glistened on his forehead. The new protective technology against the extreme weather did not stop perspiration from adrenaline, and she was sure it pumped through his veins now just as it rushed through hers.

Ace caught her attention. "We'll get 'em, Len."

She drew a long breath and met Ace's eyes. She nodded. A voice came through on Lennox's com. She raised her hand to her ear to hear it better. "We're moving in. You're clear to advance."

"Copy," Ace replied in his com before Lennox

could. "You ready?"

"Let's do this."

Before jumping down from her perch, she stole one last glance at their destination. Her heart nearly sank into her stomach as Regime soldiers shoved the Defiers into execution rows.

"They're lining them up. We have to move. We gotta go! Now!" Lennox hustled, climbing down the tree. All she could think of was that they would be too late. How terrible it was to be so close to rescuing them, only to fall short.

It had happened before. Two weeks ago.

Lennox played back the moment in her mind, recounting the horror of what she saw. They had lost them all to a firing squad. A brand-new holocaust on the horizon. One she could not seem to escape. *Not again... not today,* she promised herself.

As soon as her booted feet hit the ground, she ran alongside Ace. They did not have much time. More Sparrows ahead of them had already advanced. They remained one hundred yards apart in perimeter, covering each other's weak spots.

"Go, go, go!" She heard in her ear-piece.

Commanding her legs to move faster, she activated the Sapphire Shield in her right hand. The perfectly clear, bullet-proof sphere she had grown to love formed around her, protecting her as she pressed forward. She pulled her weapon from its holster—the Stryker filled with the Sparrow scientists' blue serum that debilitated, but could not kill.

Rage bottled up inside, but instead of focusing on its torturing fury and uncertainty, she ran toward the innocent. The detained Defiers needed them. And fast.

The earth was dry beneath her military boots and the clouds above swirled in a beautiful array of white, breaking up the solid orange-blue. The sun struck the branches with blissful light. Without the Sparrow suit on, Lennox would be pouring sweat from the heat and humidity, but adrenaline was the culprit now.

A small bead of salty liquid dripped down from her temple and ran along her cheek. Lennox tracked the other Sparrows positions on her tech watch where blue dots pinpointed their exact locations. "They're breaching the perimeter now!" Lennox shouted ahead. She and Ace were not far behind and would be entering enemy territory in less than five minutes.

As Lennox closed in, she crept toward the entrance point. Her heart thudded in her chest and courage pumped through her veins, causing her to feel purpose instead of fear. Reasons were something she never lacked.

Lennox caught up with Ace. "We need to head straight for the Defiers and escort them to the checkpoint before—"

Rapid gunfire blasted through the airwaves. *The firing squad!*

Lennox narrowed her eyes and her brows furrowed. "Hurry!"

The pair broke. Lennox headed straight for where she last saw the Defiers' rows as Ace took off toward the Regime soldiers in a high tower, whose machine guns peppered attackers with a rain of bullets. A deadly exchange of ammunition took place between the Sparrows and the Regime soldiers.

Lennox raised her shield and urged her body forward. She cast a glance upward. Ace had already climbed up the tower and was engaged in a fistfight with the two shooters.

She swallowed the lump in her throat. The scarred *D* on her arm pulsed as her heart pumped. Shots peppered her diameter. Nevertheless, she continued forward, ducking and weaving through the terrain to get to her destination, careful to avoid the rebar sticking out of the broken cement blocks. With the Sapphire Shield held ready, Lennox ran low to avoid getting shot and leapt over concrete. The sounds of war blasted all around, but her task remained clear.

Get. To. The. Survivors.

In the corner of her vision, Ace still battled the men in the high tower. She picked up speed. The Defiers were too far ahead to see clearly, but it looked like there were none left standing. She ran until she was among the fallen bodies.

The smell hit her like a tidal wave. Metal, fire, dirt, and blood. So much blood. More than she had ever seen.

Oh, God! She quivered all over and held the back of her hand to her nose. Tears fell, streaking the dirt on her cheeks.

Mothers, fathers, children. The young and the old. All were represented in a mass pile of death.

Lennox shook herself out of shock and began checking pulses. Maybe someone still lived, still breathed. She hurried up and down the rows of bodies, checking, hoping.

Lord, even if it's just one....

"Watch your six!" a voice screamed behind her.

She gaped at Ace who charged her with his weapon aimed. When it jammed, he threw it down and pulled his side arm. The bullet flew past. There was a grunt behind her followed by the heavy thud of a body hitting the dirt—proof that Ace hit his target. She'd never seen him move that fast.

She finally turned. Blood pooled from her would-be attacker's wound. Bile rose to the edge of her throat.

Thank God Ace was a good shot. She just wished it were the Sparrow bullet that hit her enemy and not the lead one in his skull. She hated seeing death, even that of her enemies. Too much of it had already consumed her world, taking her father, mother, Kira... even now, she stood in the very midst of death. It followed her like a warden of time, reminding her life was too fragile, too short and unpredictable. She was helpless against it.

Ace clenched his strong hands over her shoulders. "Are you okay?" He shook her. "Lennox, talk to me."

Lennox let out the breath in her lungs. "Fine. I'm fine." Her eyes wandered away from the blood-spill and to Ace. "Check for survivors."

"Len, there's...." Ace's hard features grew soft and he stopped.

"Just check, *please.*"

Lennox felt the weight of the world, the weight of responsibility on her shoulders. She returned to the Defiers on the ground, searching one-by-one through the rows. Every neck she held her fingers to, she removed with disappointment. Not a single person had survived. She looked to the heavens, where she acknowledged they now were, but it did not make seeing them splayed out before her, dead, any easier.

A small red sparrow twitted about. Lennox tracked it as it flew gracefully to and fro, up and down, entirely out-of-place. It chirped once before Lennox heard the shout.

"He's alive! LENNOX, HE'S ALIVE!" Ace

waved frantically.

Lennox rushed to her partner. An old man lay on his side in a heap. Lennox checked his pulse. A slow and steady thud pressed against her fingers. He *was* alive.

She gently rolled him to his back and supported his head. His concave, malnourished chest rose and fell as he took shallow, deliberate breaths. She assessed his wounds just as she had been trained to do. He had no bullet wounds to his torso, so no vital organs were damaged. Two small gashes bled from his right shoulder and one bullet-hole on his thigh. Lennox pulled out her medical kit from her pack and worked efficiently, placing a tourniquet on his upper leg and bandages on his shoulder to, at least, slow the bleeding.

The elderly man coughed.

A small smile washed Lennox's face as she inhaled her tears and gave a faint laugh. Overwhelmed, she choked out, "Thank you, God!" To hear him breathe was priceless. Lennox exhaled as everything around her turned hazy. The Sparrows overtook the rest of the Regime's stronghold. After helping two of her fellows place the survivor onto a canvas gurney, she searched for the men who were to rescue Sky. "Have you seen the Sparrow outriders?"

The two men looked up at her and shook their heads "No."

The rapid fire of machine guns echoed in the distance. Lennox bit her lip and scanned the Sparrows among the stronghold. Her eyes stopped on them—the outriders—who had searched for her best friend. They wore dirty gray camouflage uniforms and ash covered their faces from the exploding buildings behind them.

The lead Sparrow looked at her as if he knew the question she asked in her heart. He shook his head and let it fall in defeat.

They had failed. *Everyone had failed.*

Through the flames a few feet in front of her, a Regime propaganda poster hung on a wooden fence post, plastered with the face of Ahab—the man who started this war. Three words were printed on top. "Surrender. Conform. Bow."

As she fought back tears that pricked her eyes and brought pain to her chest, she furiously marched to the poster and ripped it from its place, letting it float to the ashes where it belonged. Holding back her scream, her heart wanted to stop beating, to give up the ghost that was her torn and shattered soul. But another thought took over.

Vengeance.

Chapter 3

"Alright, Sparrows, let's roll out before the Regime drones catch up to us. We can't afford to get caught up in their crossfire." Ace gripped his gun and led the way. There was no time to mourn the lost, only time to move forward and honor them by fighting to live.

Behind Lennox and the other Sparrows, the Regime stronghold burned as black smoke rose above low-lying gray clouds. Before them was a stretch of land so narrow, they almost fled in single file. The wider, vehicle capable roads were all destroyed or full of land mines. On foot was their best ticket out until they reached the Sparrow outpost where transports would meet them.

Lennox carefully stayed behind her patient as two men dragged the gurney over the uneven earth.

Ace kept everyone at a steady pace.

"How many survivors?" A tall girl with broad, strong shoulders rushed to Lennox's side, causing her to jump and clench her weapon. Her fellow Sparrow's stature was intimidating, but behind the soldier's mask, her face was that of a baby with round rosy cheeks, big bright eyes, and pink lips.

"One." Lennox maintained the pace despite the conversation.

"Just one? That's it?" The girl's voice shook.

"One is better than none." Lennox glanced at her. She had not noticed the stream of tears in the girl's eyes until now.

"All the Sparrows on my team are gone."

Lennox's stomach caught in her throat. "Gone?" How many men was it? Ten? Twelve?

Too many.

"Dead. Just like that." The weeping Sparrow shook her head and ran off ahead, flanking the other Sparrows.

Lennox wondered which peers gave up their lives this time and who would tell their families… if they had any left. Her airway tightened. It could as easily be her or Ace. The world around her moved slowly. Every tree identical to the one they passed before.

Lennox urged the others forward, trying to keep them moving at Ace's speed. "Keep up, guys! Let's go! You got this."

The war continued behind them as Sparrow outriders finished their job. The sounds of explosions filled the atmosphere.

This was nothing like training back at Sparrow City. Here, everything was too real. Real blood. Real tears. Real death. A few young Sparrows stole glances back which slowed them down.

"Don't look back. We're not going back there. Keep your eyes in the direction you want to go." Worried, tired faces met Lennox's stare. "We're gonna make it," Lennox encouraged, understanding exactly what they went through. They saw the same horrendous scene she had, and survivor's guilt could be too heavy a load for even the strongest.

The blasts echoed in the distance, growing dimmer the farther they marched. No one dared slow down again. The ground beneath their feet was fine dust and billowed into the air as their caravan moved over it.

On the day she'd lost Sky, Lennox had disabled the mainframe of the Global Weather Simulator, but she wondered if she'd been too late. Had she lost that battle, too? Even the sky cast a different hue today, one more red than pink. When the sun rose and set, it was almost the color of blood.

As Lennox ran, the tree limbs she brushed against snapped off with the slightest touch. Dry. Dead. Irreparable.

Dredging forward, silence ensued and all remained alert. But their vigilance still failed the group when a dozen rogue beasts crept out from behind several dying trees, stirring the dust beneath their paws. They were too big—unnatural, like mountain lions on growth hormones—and their eyes were like those of the genetically mutated humans.

Prowlers.

Why mutate animals now? Were the human subjects not living up to the Regime leader's expectations? Or was Ahab expanding his reach? Either way, the enhanced beasts were on the move, straight toward the Defiers.

"Lennox, do you see what I'm seeing?" Ace's voice came over on her com.

"I am. Listen, I'll distract the beasts. Get the rest of the Sparrows and our survivor to safety." Lennox turned her attention to the Sparrows. "Stay together. I'm going to try to lead them away from the group. Everything's going to be okay."

Their faces said they did not believe her.

"Stay together and get ready," she reaffirmed as she fell back, distancing herself from the crowd. If the beast was going to attack the Sparrows or her, it would be her. The lion always goes after the stray, right?

That's what Lennox was counting on, anyway.

Despite her command, the younger Sparrows scattered in mass panic while a few froze in terror at the sight of the oncoming mutated animals.

Okay, come on big fella. Look at me. She switched the ammunition in her Stryker to lethal, let out a breath, and took aim at the sky above.

Bang!

The noise carried and one of the beasts fell for her plan. It cocked its head as if deciphering her next move. It bounded toward her, as effortless as if it was created to glide over this exact terrain. Perhaps it was.

Sparrows held their weapons ready. On Ace's command, they sent a steady barrage of ammunition toward the mutant animals, unaware that Lennox successfully lured one of the lions away.

She took aim once more, lining her gun between the eyes of the mountain lion. It was just her and the beast now—one less for the others to worry about. Releasing a breath, she fired.

Bang!

The beast zagged impossibly fast, throwing itself off the direct path of the bullet. It roared, shook its head, and charged her again.

Deep breath… in and out.

She waited.

Closer, Lennox. Let him get closer.

Thirty feet and closing… twenty….

Lennox fired another round, hitting it in the chest. It did not even whimper at the shot and sprinted even faster toward her like the bullet was nothing more than a nuisance.

It was a clean shot! How? No time for

questions though. She prayed within her soul, *Jesus, help me.*

The mountain lion raced toward her.

Now!

With the animal just five feet in front of her, she pulled the trigger, hitting the mountain lion right between the eyes. The sudden impact of the bullet caused it to topple forward from its powerful momentum, flipping over itself. Its massive paws came to rest right on Lennox's chest, knocking her to the ground.

Whoosh!

Her back slammed to the earth. Air rushed out of her lungs. She wanted to panic. If it still lived, she surely wouldn't much longer. Closing her eyes and lying as still as possible, she waited to see if playing dead would help.

The mountain lion's blood dripped through the nanotubes of her suit. One drop, then another. It was like an eternity.

It's dead. It has to be.

She felt no movement, no heartbeat, no rising and falling of its chest. Lennox talked herself into getting up. Cautiously, she rolled the beast from off the top of her body. It did not fight back, nor growl.

Whew! She scrambled to her feet and poked its body with the barrel of her gun. It was dead… dead as the trees.

Lennox rushed to the crowd. The other beasts must have gone for the group. She raced to see what had become of the rest of them.

A group of Sparrows and Defiers circled around a corpse. Another mountain lion lay still at their feet. Its oversized fangs jutted from its mouth and its large paws lay limp on the ground.

Lennox forced down a sick feeling. "Anyone need a medic?" She drew attention back to reality. Someone, somewhere had to be hurt… mauled… *mutilated.* How easily the beast could have crushed any one of them in its jaws. She could barely stomach the thought. She spun in circles looking for someone to help.

Ace ran to her and grabbed her by the shoulders. "Lennox!" His dark narrowed eyes showed deep concern.

"Ace, where are they? We have to help them!"

She continued her frantic search of barely living survivors.

"Lennox, you're the one who needs the medic! Sit down," Ace commanded. "There's blood all over you. Where did it get you?"

Lennox looked down at the blood covering her jumpsuit and then waved a hand in explanation. "It's not my blood."

Ace inhaled deeply and his face softened. "Oh, thank God. I thought...."

"I'm fine. It's dead." Lennox gave a half-hearted smile to her comrade. "Thanks, Ace." He was a good friend, a good soldier.

He nodded.

Grouping everyone together again and counting a few stragglers, the lions' bodies laid sprawled out next to each other. She let out a sigh of relief when she laid eyes on her patient. He rested on the gurney, unharmed. Lennox headed toward them with Ace by her side.

Soon, the murmuring began. "So, they're using animals now too?" one of Sparrows asked, baffled.

"Looks like it," said another.

"Is anyone hurt?" Lennox asked again. She cast her glance around the crowd of dirty and tired faces. Each one shook their head.

"No, we're okay," an older Sparrow with weathered skin answered for them all.

"We should keep going, then. There could be more." Lennox looked over her shoulder past the wraithlike wilderness into an abyss of more dying foliage. "Wherever they're coming from, it isn't far," she said, scavenging the land before her.

"She's right. Let's keep moving. We have no idea what's out here." Ace readjusted the shoulder straps on his pack. "What are we waiting for? Let's move!" He clapped his hands together and took the lead again.

They forged on, desperate to reach safe land. Every now and then someone looked over their shoulder, but none dared slow down. Ungodly noises rumbled in the distance. Dry dirt crunched beneath their feet, and the wind howled through dead trees. Not even the new light of morning dulled the eeriness that surrounded them.

After a few more miles, they reached a Sparrow

outpost that marked the halfway point to their destination. Three long, round tents sat in rows—plenty of space for them all, should they stop. The tan canvas stretched over the tent poles was shredded in several places, but the constant symbol of hope—the red sparrow—was painted on the front as if brand new, untouched.

A high-ranking Sparrow held his fist in the air, halting everyone in the middle of the empty outpost. "Medics, tend to the wounded. Johnson and Parker, take watch." He motioned in the direction they were to go and finished with, "Transport for the injured will arrive at first light."

At the command, Sparrows listened and moved. Lennox overheard Ace's conversation as she obeyed.

"Sir, are you aware of the mutated mountain lions? I'm afraid this outpost may not be safe anymore." Ace tensed his jaw.

"It's as safe as we can be right now." The Sparrow General placed a hand on Ace's shoulder before he walked off.

Ace's gaze fell on Lennox. She smiled, trying to reassure him the best she could, and then rounded up anyone with injuries to escort them to the first tent.

"Can I help?" Ace caught up to her. "Staying busy helps... *you know*...."

"I know." Lennox understood exactly what he felt. The need to be useful, the need to be distracted from what they had all just seen, busy hands tempered anxious minds. "We can always use an extra pair of hands. Why don't you help bring in the injured?"

Ace nodded. "I will." His brows drew together. "Thanks."

"Of course." Lennox took a deep, slow breath to cleanse her own mind from everything she could not control, everything out of her hands... like the heartbreak of Sky's absence.

She moved to her post. A few Sparrows sat holding their heads in their hands as they mourned, while others washed blood and dirt off their faces. Most of the injured had lacerations that needed stitches. A simple fix that other medics could tend to. As Lead Medic, Lennox focused on the patient that was not going to be so easy.

The old man, the lone survivor of the execution, rested on a cot bloodied from a previous occupant. He still wore the standard tan prisoner jumpsuit the Regime had supplied all of their prisoners. The fabric almost swallowed him whole.

She studied him as he slept, tracking his vitals and calculating his chance of survival. His face contorted in pain, yet moans avoided his lips. He had lost all coloring and had experienced repeated sessions of dry heaves until the veins in his forehead protruded. Blood rushed to his ashen face.

Lord, help this man and keep the Regime at bay, at least long enough for us to regain our forces. I know You have a plan. Help us to accomplish it.

With the close of her prayer, Lennox noticed the old man's eyes flit open. She bent down, preparing her medical kit. "My name's Lennox. I'm a Sparrow medic. I'm here to help. What's your name?" The question was automatic, rehearsed, but sincere. She wanted to call each patient by name, to let them know she saw a person and not just a patient. They had lives, family, friends… they loved, they feared, and they mourned. And they were all in this together. That's what she wanted them to know—she was in it with them.

The man coughed a bit before replying. "Charles, but my friends call me Chuck."

"Okay, Chuck, I am going to take a look, all right?"

"Sure, go right on ahead, dear." His voice was low and hoarse.

Lennox took him in. Dry, pale skin, sunken eyes, cracked lips, all the signs of severe dehydration. "First, an IV drip okay?" She rolled up his sleeve and rubbed her hand over his bony arm to feel his veins. She could not decide which was worse, his malnourishment or his gunshot wound.

"Okay," Chuck gave a wrinkled smile.

His eyes were fearless, even after all he had encountered. Light still beamed from his soul. The elderly man reminded her so much of Sky's late grandfather. She could not help Pop, but she could help Chuck. And, she would, with everything within her.

She put on her gloves and worked. Lennox cut the tan jumpsuit fabric back from the wound. Taking the instant numbing spray out that the Sparrow scientists had created, she applied a generous amount to the wound. Chuck winced at its coolness and then relaxed.

"Feel a little better?" She softened her gaze and curved her lips slightly upwards.

"Much," he nodded. The wrinkles in his skin bunched together.

She reached in her kit for the surgical pliers and held them firmly in her hands. No operating rooms here, no real doctors. It was just her and a few other combat medics getting the job done.

She inhaled. *Steady....*

Placing the medical pliers in the wound, she searched for the bullet. Gently, she dug deeper into the pierced flesh until the metal surgical utensil clinked against the lodged bullet. The opening gushed and she held the gauze at the edge of it with her left hand as she secured the foreign object in between the pliers.

"Got it," she said, holding it up. She threaded a needle and sewed his pale, stretched out skin back together and applied the rapid healing medication on it—the same medication a different medic had used on her shoulder a few months ago. Her shoulder felt brand new already, so she hoped his leg would too, eventually. At his age, she was not sure. She wasn't even sure how he made it this far.

As she finished wrapping up the wound, she smiled at her patient. "All done."

Chuck reached out for Lennox's hand. His cold fingers wrapped around hers. "Thank you for not leaving me behind." His sincere gratitude poured onto the features of his face, eyes gleaming. "Many would, you know."

Lennox wanted to cry at the thought of Chuck being left behind by anyone. "We Defiers have to stick together." She gave him a warm smile as she gathered her supplies and then rested a hand on Chuck's shoulder. "I will be back to check on you in a little bit."

"I look forward to it." Chuck lifted his hand, placing it on top of hers and patted.

On her way out of the tent for a breath of fresh air, Lennox nodded to her fellow medics. The metallic smell of blood became too much sometimes. As she looked at the reddened moon that was visible even with the mid-afternoon sun, she thought of how far God had brought them all—how far He had brought her. Sparrows bustled about, back and forth as she took inventory of her world.

There was much more work to be done, and today, as crazy as it was, was just another day in the life of a Sparrow—*her life*.

Chapter 4

At 9 p.m., a voice came over the intercom, blasting throughout the Sparrow camp. "All available units report to the strategy tent . . . all available units report to the strategy tent . . ."

Lennox followed her peers to the tent that sat to the north of the medical post, asking the man beside her, "Hey, do you know what's going on?"

He shook his head and glanced her way. "Not a clue, but I know it's not good. It's never good when they call us all in." He faced forward again and continued walking.

Sparrows from the outer perimeter joined them and everyone walked to the worn-down strategy tent. Lennox scanned the crowd as she stepped in. She recognized a few faces from the mission, others she remembered from Sparrow City.

Ace found a place beside her. "What's going on?"

Lennox looked into his deep brown eyes and shrugged. "I don't know."

Soon, several high-ranking Sparrows entered and stood in front of all the uniformed men and women.

"When did they get here?" Lennox asked.

Ace raised his brows. "No idea."

One of the Sparrow leaders placed a hologram portal on a table and explained as images filled the area around them. "As some of you may already know, the northern regions of the United States have already been fully claimed by Ahab and the Regime. Now...." His voice cracked. He held a hand to his lips and coughed, seeming to fight back tears. "Now, they are using chemical warfare just north of us, only one hundred miles from right where we stand."

Three-dimensional images of defiant cities cast enough vivid color to light up faces nearby. It was like the videos and images displayed at training camp in Sparrow City to prepare the Sparrows' hearts for war and more disturbing truths. The portal displayed crowds of people who frantically covered their faces as planes above dropped chemical bombs. As soon as the canisters touched the ground, lethal gases dispersed. The screams were so ear-piercing some Sparrows winced, including Lennox, but she forced herself to watch. She witnessed the death of the innocent to fuel the fire within her very being. Heat rushed every part of her body as she saw men, women, and children vainly hold their hands over their mouths and noses, only to drop to their knees, and then fully to the ground. Bodies convulsed, and one-by-one, they died painful, terrible deaths.

As that hologram video finished, another one began. Another city. Another crowd. More pain, destruction, and death. Threads of anger and sorrow weaved around every inch of her soul, casting a shadow of darkness upon her thoughts. Everything within her suffocated—her heart, her thoughts, her lungs. They could not grasp the breath they needed—like the crowd she just saw. She was dying inside, a little bit more with each heartrending scene.

Yet another video played… and another… and

another. She stopped counting after eight. The faces of Defiers blended together and she hated it. She wanted to remember each one of their precious spirits. She wanted to know their names, to keep their memory alive, and to remember their sacrifice…their bravery.

The Sparrow at the front continued. "Over a dozen defiant Texas cities have been annihilated by Ahab's orders, and that number is growing daily. One of our drones captured footage of Ahab traveling through these cities after the gases subside to make sure the job was done right. He films his gruesome victories and releases it on all the newsfeeds throughout the world."

A new hologram video played. In the midst of corpses, Ahab posed in a self-righteous stance with his arms folded over his chest as his face looked up victoriously for a still-shot—as if he made the world a better place by ridding it of anyone who disagreed with him. "Religion is a disease," the Regime leader's voice came through the portal. "And there is none more tainted and viral than Christianity. We must absolve ourselves from their existence once and for all to truly have the peace we seek."

Lennox cringed. *Peace? What peace?*

The Lead Sparrow caught her attention with his own words, breaking up the utter heartache she felt which caused her blood to boil. "Ahab's objective is clear. He aims to create chaos and horror to get the remaining defiant cities to bow. As of right now, we have Sparrows on the ground and in the air in pursuit of Ahab. Our focus here must remain on securing Defiers and getting them to safety. Any questions?"

Lennox stormed out the back exit of the tent and held in her screams, raising her hands over her head and resting them on top. She could not take it anymore!

Ace rushed to her side. "Ahab is controlled by the devil himself, isn't he? I can't stand to see those holograms. I just want to reach through the images and protect all of them, you know?" he sniffled.

Lennox turned toward her friend, her heart on fire with unrelenting pain. "Are we doing enough?" She waited for an answer but only got Ace's panged stare, so she asked the questions that had been burning holes in her soul. "I mean, when does it end? When we're all dead?" She shook her head and lowered her hands to her side, digging her nails deep into her palms. "When will Ahab finally pay for all he's done?"

Ace faced her. "You sound like me now. If I remember clearly, it wasn't too long ago that you told me to try to forgive them."

A tear rolled down Lennox's cheek. "Sometimes I don't feel like forgiving. Sometimes... sometimes all I feel is the need to avenge my parents, my friends—"

"And Sky." Ace placed his hands in his pockets.

Lennox looked up, trying to keep any more tears from falling. "And Sky," she confirmed. She met Ace's eyes again. "Here it is, the end of the world, and all I wish is that things were normal again. Go to college, get married to Sky...." She let out a small laugh. "And have kids one day that looked just like him. And I know that's crazy—that we won't get our happily ever after on earth and I have to be okay with that... come to terms with it somehow... but how can I live knowing he may very well spend eternity in hell? I *have* to know he's okay. Does that make me selfish?"

Ace shook his head. "No, it makes you human."

Chapter 5

Lennox stretched, sitting at the edge of her cot as other Sparrows moved about the tent. Only hints of the early morning light shone through its seams and rips.

One by one, the night crew shuffled to their designated cots and plastered their bodies to them, their exhaustion clear. They had been up all night, keeping watch. The Regime could be lurking just outside of camp, ready and waiting to strike. The enemy always snuck around like the slithering snake it was.

Lennox squeezed her eyes tight and reopened, adjusting her vision. She leaned over and grabbed her gear, glancing at the sound of a familiar hum. Sparrow vehicles pulled up outside. Transport had arrived.

Quickly sliding her feet through the gray jumpsuit pants, she stood and slid her arms into the sleeves. She attached her Sparrow gun around her thigh and zipped the jumpsuit up over her tights. Bending down, she laced her boots up and was ready to move out into the open. It wasn't safe and they were like open targets to the enemy. She secured her weapons once more, gritted her teeth, and walked out to help guide the Defiers onto the correct transports.

The sun flickered past thirsty trees. Its blinding light was different than before, but no matter on which side of the world Sky stood, Lennox always held onto the thought that he saw the same light of the sun, whether it be direct or reflected. He still saw it, just like her, and knowing that made life a little bit easier.

Yet, she still scolded herself. Maybe she *was* too late destroying the GWS' mainframe. Earth seemed as if it enveloped itself within its own misery. Even what was left of the surviving animals wallowed in discomfort. Guilt lay heavy on her shoulders. All the "would haves," "could haves," and "should haves" rolled over and over her thoughts.

She could not change that now, though, and had to remind herself—sometimes daily—that none of this was her fault. She wasn't the one who started the war, but, oh, how she longed to be among those who ended it.

She entered the recovery tent where she was glad to see Chuck sitting up, smiling.

"Good morning, Chuck," she greeted him.

"Good morning, dear."

"Someone is up bright and early this morning."

"Just got done praying." Chuck lifted his uninjured arm off his lap and down again, shaking his head. "You know, we are all really waiting for that blessed hope God promised us. I never thought I'd live to see the day of His Second Coming, but it looks like I just may."

At the realization that Jesus could return soon—any minute really—Lennox paused a moment before speaking again. "That's going to be a great day, isn't it?"

Chuck tilted his head back and breathed in deeply as a wide grin spread across his face. His smile reached all the way to his eyes. "A great day, indeed, dear. A great day, indeed."

"Well, while we wait on Him, how about we get you out of here?"

She checked his vitals, flashing a small light at his pupils, and then monitored his heart rate. His bandages were fresh and already taken care of. The other Sparrows must have monitored him closely through the night.

"Let's get you in this wheelchair, shall we?" Lennox helped him to a sitting position and wrapped his good arm around her shoulders, then eased him into the chair. The purr of an engine right outside the medical tent made her look up. "Good. The first med Humvee has arrived. I'll be sure you're the first on it."

"Thank you." Chuck rested his old, wrinkled hand on her arm. The corners of his eyes creased even more as his smile widened.

Lennox smiled back and lowered her head with honor. "Anytime."

She walked outside to greet her fellow medics and was met by a young man wearing a medic uniform. His dark brown eyes and tanned skin were warm and welcoming.

Lennox stuck out her hand to introduce herself. "Lennox."

He returned the gesture. "Logan."

They headed toward the tent. Lennox led him inside to where Chuck patiently waited.

"Chuck, this is Logan." Lennox tensed her jaw, realizing she would most likely never see Chuck again. He would go his way and she would go hers. She ignored the heartache and continued. "He's going to take good care of you on the ride to a safer Sparrow post."

"Oh, I'm sure he will, dear." He grabbed hold of her hand once more. "I'll be fine," he pointed at her, "and so will you."

Lennox nodded in agreement, bent down, and gave him one last hug goodbye. She would always remember this sole survivor. But as the Sparrow transport medic exited with Chuck, Lennox saw a flash of something—or *someone*—out of the corner of her eye, distracting her.

The canvas slit flapped back and forth with the wind. A lump formed in her throat. She drew her handgun from her thigh holster, not sure if it was just a wild animal, but not taking any chances. Walking outside, she crept toward the movement she swore she saw.

Am I going mad? Paranoia wasn't uncommon when every single day you had the chance of being attacked. *Deep breath.*

She scanned the grounds, where Sparrows moved in and out of canvas tents. Only dead trees and brush provided cover near the outskirts, so whatever it was did not have many options to hide behind without being seen by at least one person.

She turned back, but something in her would not let her leave. Her senses heightened and her heart beat hard against her ribcage. She heard the thud in her ears until another noise caught her attention.

Snap!

One dead twig was all it took. Lennox spun around on her heel with her weapon raised and finger on the trigger.

"Whoa! Whoa! Whoa!" Ace raised his hands in a surrendered gesture. "Lennox! What are you doing?" He placed his left hand on her weapon to lower it from his face, keeping his right slightly raised.

"Geez, Ace!" she exhaled. "I could have killed you!" Lennox dropped her arms and now held the weapon at her side.

"Yeah, I see that, but I would have been fine. I have my Kev disk on." He examined her suit and quickly noticed she did not. "You should too! What in the world are you doing out here?"

Lennox placed the small disk on her sleeve and activated it. The bulletproof technology formed around her. Ace's jawline relaxed and his furrowed brows returned to normal. Lennox never knew him to be much of a stickler for the rules. She headed back to her tent.

Ace followed. "What'd you see out there, anyway?" He looked over his shoulder with brows furrowed. He glanced back and forth throughout the dead forest of half-fallen trees.

"I don't know. Maybe nothing." Lennox quickened her pace as she returned the gun to her holster and snapped the strap over it.

Ace threw out his hand and grasped her sleeve, which made her stop. "You sure have been on edge lately. I mean, we all are, but you... you are more than usual." His dark eyes narrowed as he cocked his head.

She slid him a guarded look. "Yeah, it's nothing. We're all on edge." Lennox stared at Ace's endearing face and posed a question she already knew the answer to. "Aren't you?"

Ace bit his lower lip as if he searched for the answer. "I mean, of course. Len, it's war. War is ugly... *nasty.* You know this more than anyone. With your parents... and your friend, Kira—"

"I know." She thought back to the video of her parents' murders—a flowy dress, her dad's hand reaching for her mother's, a man forcing them to their knees.

Two gunshots.

Bile rose in her throat. She knew. She remembered standing by Kira's bedside as life slipped from her best friend's body and into eternity.

"I know." She raised both hands to her hips and frowned. Tears welled in her eyes. She missed her mom, dad, and Kira so much. They didn't deserve to die by the hands of the Regime like they had.

Fight.

The word was as crystal-clear in her spirit as the first time she heard her parents say it in her dream. The only way through the Regime was to push back harder. She could not bring her parents or Kira back, but she could bring Sky back.

If I can find him. Lennox sighed, noticing Ace stood quietly, watching her as she thought.

"Uh-hum." Ace cleared his throat and swerved the topic. "Colonel is rounding everyone up. We have new orders. We're reassigned to patrolling the flanks on the bikes with Stevens and Cassidy. You ready?"

"Ready."

She was always ready.

Mounting the Sparrow motorcycle, Lennox could not help but think about Sky. Then again, could she ever help it? She always had him on her conscience. How could she have let them pull her away to safety while Sky was being buried alive by rubble? The memories stung like a thousand angry hornets.

Focus, Lennox. She'd promised herself she would not let her regret interfere with her duties. She still had a responsibility to uphold. Others depended on her... counted on her. She'd be there for them as they needed her to be. She would not fail. Not now.

No matter what.

She placed her helmet over her head and the

protective, self-shaping nanotubes from the Kev disk soon worked their way around it, furthering her protection from a barrage of artillery—should it come. She turned on the silent bike the Sparrow scientists referred to as a "Vanisher." She realigned her focus even more as she rode into position alongside the Humvee. Ace and Cassidy took the front flanks as Lennox and Stevens took their place on both sides of the back.

Traveling to the base of operations, they avoided roads and maintained their pace on barren, dry land. The hue above them was an ominous mixture of brown, red, and orange. No buzzards. No insects. Not even one lone bird was in the sky, now. Clouds failed to make their appearance, and these sunny days matched what Lennox imagined another planet to be like. She missed the pure blue that used to mix in the skies. For now, earth was unearthly. The rusty colors swirled together in a dance as an angry cloud instantly formed. Flashes of lightning bounced from one end of the earth to the other. Lennox thought it could all fall apart at any moment.

Setting her sights before her, she gripped the

handles of her bike as the engine vibrated against her hands. She held on tight, maneuvering the all-terrain tires over the dusty ground. The Humvees created a tan fog as they kicked up the dry dirt around them. Lennox rubbed the outside of her visor with the back of her hand to remove the caked on dust. She squinted and swerved from behind the main convoy to keep her sightline open as much as possible.

Several uneventful miles passed before Lennox saw movement in her peripheral vision again. She looked to her right. A genetically altered mountain lion galloped effortlessly no more than thirty feet from her—completely entranced. Lennox did not dare slow her bike or leave her position open, so she kept pace with the caravan as the lion lurked closer.

She spoke over her com to the others. "Hey, you guys seeing what I'm seeing?"

They answered one-by-one.

"I don't see anything."

"What you got?"

"Lennox?"

Lennox glanced to the front and then back again. She found a glowing pair of human—yet inhuman—eyes staring back at her.

A Prowler!

Chills ran down her spine. Steadying her bike with one hand, she prepared to un-holster her weapon with the other and readied herself for a fight, but the genetically advanced man went after the mountain lion instead.

This doesn't seem right. Why would....

She focused on the inhuman eyes again. They were familiar... somehow... even while they glowed.

She gasped. *Sky?*

"Lennox!" a flustered voice shouted through the com.

She double checked her surroundings to confirm what happened. This was it! This one moment was what she waited for. She glanced back.

Nothing.

She searched for the Prowler fighting the mountain lion, but they were both gone. Had she imagined it all?

Impossible. It was too real. She saw them. Both of them! Her heart beat faster until her nerves shook. She wanted to scream, to ask God to take away these cruel, false glimpses of the one she loved, for they only teased her soul.

"Lennox, come in. Do you copy?"

With a deep breath, she stole one more glance. Still nothing.

"False alarm." Lennox's voice betrayed her and exposed her inward sorrow. She felt like a little girl again, imagining monsters that were not there. It was one thing to see shadows in her dreams, but hallucinating while awake was worse. Maybe everything was finally catching up with her.

She needed to get her head straight. She needed God to work in her brokenness before she fell apart completely.

Chapter 6

They all arrived safely to the Sparrow post at lunchtime. Lennox sat at a table in the Mess Hall. The tan canvas flapped with every breeze. This Mess Hall wasn't securely underground like the one in Sparrow City. It was a simple, round tent where Sparrows ate. They served stew today, but Lennox could not eat after the rough morning. She pushed the deer meat, potatoes, and carrots around the brown seasoned broth until the steam quit rising from it and it grew cold.

God, where could he be? Why do I keep on seeing him everywhere? Come on, Lennox, pull yourself together.

"Heard you all had another successful rescue mission today." The calming voice of her brother broke through her inner dialogue. Oliver sat right in front of

Lennox on the opposite side of the table.

"Huh? Oh, yeah. We did, thank God!" Lennox forced herself to quit stirring her food around.

"Hey, you okay?" He lifted an eyebrow. War had aged his handsome face. A scruffy beard covered his jawline and the sun leathered the skin on his forehead.

Lennox met his gaze, gave him a half-smile, and nodded.

"I know that silence is a coping mechanism for you sometimes." He paused for a brief second and gave her a reassuring look. "I know that you're still struggling with losing Sky. I am too. We all are."

Losing. She hated that word and what it really meant when someone said it. They had said it to her at her parents' graveside, "*I'm sorry for your loss.... My condolences for your loss....*" Lennox studied her brother's hazel eyes. "That's just it. Sky's only lost, not gone. I know he's still out there somewhere. Fighting to be himself again." She looked her brother square in the face. "He's not dead."

Oliver seemed taken aback. "You're still holding out hope he's alive after the last mission?"

"Yes, of course I am holding onto hope. You're the one who told me to trust God and not to lean on my own understanding. I don't understand, and I don't have to." She thought about it before she spoke, careful to choose her words wisely. "I'm positive he's alive. I can feel it."

"Len, after last time, I just… I just don't want you to hold out hope and then be crushed by any news—"

"Oliver, he's alive. I know it."

Oliver's Adam's apple bobbed. "Okay, then I'll hold onto hope right alongside you." He covered her hand with his own and squeezed tight. "Never lose faith, right?"

"Right." Lennox managed a sincere smile. "Thanks, Oli." She had not called him that since she was little and was unable to pronounce his full name, but it felt right in this moment. He would always be her protective big brother, protecting her both physically and emotionally. She loved him for it.

His gaze softened. He released her hand. "Hey, when you're done eating you should come visit Sia and Max."

Lennox perked up at the mention of the two Sparrow scientists' names. "They're here?"

"Yeah, we had to pull them out of Sparrow City, which was nearly impossible due to the Regime's presence all around there now. It's not safe to enter and exit by ground any more, and barely by air. We brought Sia and Max here to see if they can build more domes around other safe zones to make more impenetrable cities—cities the Regime doesn't know about—so we can protect more Defiers. I'm sure they'd love to see you."

"I'd love to see them! I miss them, actually." The friendly banter between Sia and Max always brightened Lennox's day. She took one bite of cold stew to avoid questions about her appetite, and stood. "I'm done. Can we go see them right now?"

Oliver stared at her bowl. "Not hungry?"

"No." Lennox should have known her brother was too observant when it came to her, but he let it drop.

Oliver led Lennox out of the Mess Hall to another recently erected tent. The spotless canvas with the red sparrow at the top center of the A-line framed structure was pristine. He held the canvas apart as they walked through. Inside was a makeshift science lab full of tools, computers, and wires.

Max saw her first. "Lennox!" He ran to embrace her with an awkward hug, one only he could give. His red hair lay disheveled on top of his head and dark circles sat underneath his green eyes.

"Hi, Max. Good to see you." It was so comforting to be in the company of her scientist friend again. The weight on her heart lifted, even if for a little bit, it was nice.

"Good to see you too! Sia, come see who it is." Max waited patiently for a whole ten seconds. "SIA! Quit tinkering and come see who came to visit us!" He lowered his voice to a whisper. "Sorry, you know how she is, always working so seriously."

A frustrated sigh came from the back. Before they saw the spunky short-haired scientist, they heard her.

"Max, you know I am working and I lose my train of thought when you yell at me!" Her spiky dark hair was all that peeked through the rows of metal shelves as she headed their way. She passed a table full of gadgets and turned the corner. Her face lit up and the wrinkles left her forehead when she saw Lennox and Oliver. "Oh! Sorry, guys. I'm not trying to be rude. Max, here, just annoys the living fire out of me." She wiped her hands on the white lab coat she wore and reached out to shake hands.

Their different greetings summed them up perfectly. Max—the hugger. Sia—the firm hand shake.

Oliver took her hand, shaking it firmly, twice. "I thought maybe you two could show Lennox some of the new technology you have been working on since I'm sure she will be using it on rescue missions, soon."

Max jumped and squeezed his fists to his chest as if so excited to have a show-and-tell. "Of course, we can!"

Sia rolled her eyes. "Just be sure you work out the kinks before you have them try something this time, please." Sia shook her head. "This knuckle-head," she pointed to Max, "gave a prototype to one of the trainees to try out and it exploded. It nearly knocked the kid out!"

"What! *Noooo...*" Max protested. "It merely smoked... *a little*." He gave Lennox a wink.

"Whatever you say."

"Okay, Ms. Smartie Pants, tell them who invented this!" Max held up what looked like a silver bullet.

With a slow breath she said, "You did." Then she smiled and gave him an elbow to the ribs.

"Ouch!"

Oliver lowered his mouth to Lennox's ear. "It's like the three stooges, only one's missing," he laughed.

"And they're a lot smarter."

"Yeah, that too." The corners of Oliver's mouth curved slightly upward. "You'll love this invention." He nudged Lennox's side.

"Introducing the all new Personal Dome." Max activated the tech and it flickered into position around him and whoever stood close by, which in his case, was Sia.

"I have to hand it to you, Max. It's brilliant." Sia pursed her lips in jest.

"Go ahead, try to come in," Max challenged.

Lennox took a step forward. Oliver pulled her back. "Uh, Max, I don't think my sister wants that jolt of voltage today."

"Oh, right, right. What was I thinking?" Max scrunched his Irish features together.

"See?" Sia crossed her arms. "You have to be more careful!"

Max pressed the silver bullet-shaped tech again and the protective sphere dissolved. "So yeah. It's a barrier that protects those within it from immediate threat of danger, much like the Kev disk I made for the Sparrows, but it has a broader reach. Think of it as a scaled down version of the dome around Sparrow City." Max handed her the technology. It felt warm to the touch. "It's warm because of the electric current." Max smiled. "You can keep that one."

Lennox's eyes wandered to Sia, seeking permission.

"I'm afraid not. I swear Max can't keep a lid on any of his projects. We are making more, hopefully enough for everyone to have one of their own that works perfectly, *without* any flaws. The only real problem with them is that they can only sustain the personal dome for a few minutes at a time. It's not fail proof, but it is better than nothing. That's what I'm working on now—sustaining it."

"I understand," Lennox said, giving the technology back to its creator.

"Sorry," Max shrugged.

"It's really okay. I'm sure I'll get one when they're ready," Lennox smiled.

An emergency siren sounded and lights flashed in the scientists' tent.

"What's going on?" Lennox asked.

"Weather disruptions." Max swallowed hard.

"Even with the Global Weather Simulator destroyed, the earth has lost its rhythm. The GWS caused enough damage to alter everything, even with it out of commission," Sia explained and headed straight for her station.

Max clasped Lennox's hands and looked her straight in her eyes. "It was really good to see you, my friend, but duty calls." He released her and winked, mouthing the words "Keep it," and then scurried to his post.

When Lennox opened her right hand, she saw the Personal Dome technology. She closed a tight fist around it.

Oliver reached out and touched Lennox's

shoulder. "We better leave them to their work."

Lennox agreed and waved goodbye to the preoccupied scientists. They waved back hastily, returning to their tasks.

A lump formed in her throat. The devastating impact of the GWS was still in effect, even after its destruction.

She *was* too late.

Chapter 7

Lennox parted ways with Oliver and headed for the Triage Tent under the orange-red sky. The cracked land was dry, with patches of dying grass and weeds, but after the hectic alarms and flashing of lights in the makeshift science lab, the open, outside air refreshed her, even with everything visually different.

Maybe she was needed there. She fiddled with the tiny silver piece of tech Max gave her, passing it between her fingers. *Maybe busy hands will occupy my brain, as well.* Probably not, but it was worth a shot. She'd try anything to keep her dark thoughts from invading reality.

As she tucked the tech away in her cargo-pants' pocket, she watched the women sitting with their children outside their tents. Their faces were dirty and clothes, torn, but still they smiled. It made Lennox think about how it had been worth it to become a Sparrow and do what she did. *For them.* She did it for them and everyone like them.

Snap!

Lennox swore she saw dust rise when she heard the sound, but she'd been wrong before. Many times. She chose to ignore this time to keep herself from looking like a fool. She hated to repeat past mistakes. She wanted to learn from every single one of them, so this time she did. She walked forward. Two more tents and she'd reach her destination.

Snap!

"That's it!" Lennox pulled up her Stryker and headed toward the noise. *I can't be going crazy. Can I?*

Lennox inched closer. One step and then another until she found herself alone in the woods. She stopped. She was too far away from everyone else. Unsettled dust wafted in the air. Someone or something was just there, literally seconds before. Who could move that fast? Her heart skipped a beat.

Sky could.

With the Regime's genetically mutating Venom

in his veins, he moved faster than humanly possible. She remembered how quickly he carried her up the stairwell of the imploding building the Regime had bombed. He got her to safety when no one else had the power. It had to be him.

At least that was what she hoped. That's what she always hoped.

Lennox wanted to call out for him, but a voice in the back of her mind told her that would be unwise. That gut-wrenching feeling told her to stop, to go back.

Don't press forward, don't move on, go back... Go! Back! It was as if someone screamed the words in her mind, but it wasn't her voice.

She reluctantly ignored the inner caution and searched the area for two more minutes, gun steady, senses alert.

Then it all made sense.

A stranger appeared from behind the trees like a ghost through a wall and stood too close. She sucked in a breath as if someone stole the oxygen right out from her lungs. He wore the Regime's infamous black fatigues with the emblem of a snake poised to strike— like Sky would possibly have on, but his build was

71

slightly different and his eyes were off... *way off.* No. This wasn't Sky, but the enemy.

She pulled the trigger without hesitation, but the man shoved her hands with animalistic strength and caused her to miss. Lennox searched for her much-needed weapon and found it on the ground a few feet away. She lifted her hands and clenched them into tight fists before she threw a right hook into his jaw. The reverberation sent splintering pain through her knuckles.

Who... no... what is this guy?

The Regime soldier responded by trying to crush his arm down over her face. She blocked his blow last-second with her forearm and put a fist right in his face again. She shoved her knee into his ribs as hard as possible. It fazed him, slightly, but he seemed more amused by her efforts, like he was letting her get in hits.

Frustrated, Lennox charged. The man side stepped, shoving her as she passed him. *Uh!* Lennox spun back around and balanced herself. By no means was she weak, she had trained for this. She had the skillset, but this man was something beyond her training.

As the soldier lowered his head, an evil grimace spread across his face. He lunged and reached out, spinning her around with one effortless movement. He let out a satisfied laugh as he held her in a chokehold. Her hands flew up and grasped his muscular forearms, trying to release the pressure they held around her neck.

"Not bad for a female," he whispered into her ear.

Pig. His words sent fury through her limbs. She kicked, trying to lash out with her arms and legs, but he held her tight. She should have listened to the still, small voice that warned her. It had to be God. Why didn't she listen?

Fight. She recognized her parents' voices in her head now. Her training kicked in and she remembered the practice she had with her brother only weeks before. "Fight using their own strength as a weapon against them," Oliver used to coach her while she trained with larger Sparrows.

She struggled through the cloudiness of lack of oxygen, tucked her chin, and leaned into the chokehold. She bore down on his grasp with her arms, throwing him off balance, and then thrust her head back into his face.

He cursed as his grasp loosened enough for her to wiggle free. She whirled around and jabbed a knee into his side, along with a fist to his already bloodied nose. He threw himself forward, tackling her like a linebacker.

"Oof!" He knocked the breath from her lungs. With her back against the dirt, she shoved his chest up with her arms and wrapped her legs around his torso, trying to pressure him off her stomach. Struggling, she scanned the ground for her gun. There it was, barely out of reach.

The Regime soldier tried to unwrap Lennox's legs from around his ribs. She squeezed her thighs harder, wishing to control the direction in which they moved. She inched herself closer to her weapon with every spare centimeter of wiggle room.

Just a little bit farther.

"Aahh!" She cried out through gritted teeth. *Come on!*

Her fingers crawled in the dust, beckoning the strength to stretch out a little more.

Almost....

Reaching with her right hand and fending off the attacks with the other, she grabbed the gun and struck the man on his temple. He rolled just enough for her to shove him off her stomach. She bolted to her feet, but the Regime soldier was already upright.

She raised the weapon, aiming at his chest. "Don't you dare move!" It would be so easy to click the switch on the Stryker to lethal ammunition and end him like he had most likely ended so many other lives.

Blood dripped down her cheek to her lips, leaving a metallic taste behind. Her finger rested on the button as she wavered between two fates.

"How old are you, darling?" the Regime soldier asked. "What, seventeen? Maybe eighteen? This war is…" Something stole his attention. His head tilted like a dog's, trying to make out what was before him and behind Lennox. "Saraya?" the man asked with a hint of confusion in his voice. He appeared to recognize whom he saw.

Saraya. Who's Saraya?

Lennox took a split-second glimpse over her shoulder, but he took advantage and moved forward.

She fired without hesitation and he dropped like a star out of the sky. She stared at the man who had her in his vice. His veins glowed blue and his fingers contorted as his face mirrored the pain he surely felt.

Sparrow ammunition at its finest—not lethal, but efficient.

"Good work, Lennox."

"Captain Easton?" Lennox spun around, perplexed. "You know him?"

Easton pinned the man with her eyes and a line etched between her brows. "Unfortunately, yes. His name's Tomas." The Sparrow Captain helped Lennox raise the enemy to his feet. "He is not a good man. Sometimes, I wish God did not give second chances. But then, where would I be?" Easton seemed to speak more to herself than to Lennox. She shook her head and made eye contact. "You okay?"

Lennox raised her hands above her head and rested them on top to try to regulate her breathing. "Yeah, I'm fine." She wiped the blood running down her face with the back of her hand. "It was stupid of me to come this far alone. I just thought…." Now was not the time. "Never mind."

Easton patted Lennox on the shoulder and secured restraints on Tomas. "I'm going to let the serum run in him for a bit. Hopefully he's the only one out here. I'll check him for trackers and call it in." Easton pressed her com. "Send a team to survey the perimeter to make sure it's secure, we've got a Regime scout over here on the northwest side of base." Easton returned her attention back to Lennox. "Hopefully Max and Sia will have a dome over this place soon."

"Yeah, let's hope so." Lennox desperately wanted to ask about the man, Tomas. "Easton?" Lennox waited, curious, but nervous about being too intrusive.

"You're going to ask how the soldier knew me, aren't you?"

Lennox nodded. "He called you Saraya. I've never heard anyone call you that. Is that your first name?" Lennox had only known Easton as Captain Easton, nothing more, nothing less. Easton was the only moniker anyone ever called her. Why had she never thought to ask her first name? She felt rude now for not knowing more about her leader, but maybe that's how Easton wanted it.

"Yes, but I don't tell very many people that. Only your brother and Eli know. I don't want that to be what people call me." Easton licked her dry lips. "We better get this guy to a cell."

Heaving the man to his feet, Easton commanded him forward. He could not fight against the serum, although he seemed to try. He was forced to obey the request, however painful. Sparrow recruits often wondered what was in the concoction the scientists created. Lennox had been a party to many late-night discussions about it, but no one knew what made it work.

Lennox cleared her throat and persisted as they walked with their prisoner back to the base. "It's a beautiful name." Lennox paused to see if Easton would acknowledge her when she brought it up again.

Easton simply gave a tilt of her head.

That was enough to encourage Lennox to press more. She hated that she was so curious and asked the maybe too personal question before she thought twice. "Why wouldn't you want anyone to call you that?"

"Where I am from, it means princess." Easton kept her face straightforward and kept the pace.

"Isn't that a good thing?" Lennox eyed her.

The prisoner managed a small huff.

Easton shoved him forward, daring him to step out of line. "Almost there, Tomas. Don't cause yourself any more trouble."

Tomas groaned, but heeded the warning.

Two male Sparrows relieved Easton of her burden as they arrived at base. He mumbled phrases in another language as they dragged him away.

A tear streamed down Easton's face and she quickly wiped it away. "Come, I'll tell you everything." She motioned for Lennox to follow her to the Mess Hall. "Do you mind getting me some water, please?"

The Sparrow captain took a seat at an empty picnic-style table as Lennox grabbed bottles of water for them both. Easton took a sip and, with a heavy sigh, continued on the topic as if they never took a break from it.

"It *is* a beautiful name, but for me, the name comes with very hard memories, terrible memories. Memories I wish I could forget." She paused for a moment, as if unsure of how to proceed. "Lennox, I

have not always been this person you see today. I...
uh...." Easton took a deep breath and looked up to the
top of the tent and back down. "I was a Regime soldier
over in the Eastern countries, where Ahab took over
first."

Shock resonated in Lennox's brain as she
waited for Easton to continue.

"Ahab had just started making Prowlers and
wanted to experiment on a female soldier, so I...
volunteered."

"You *volunteered* to become a Prowler?"
Lennox was speechless after she released those words.
Her mouth was agape and her heart skipped a beat.
Why would anyone volunteer to be made into a
monster?

"I was a lost girl, an empty soul." Easton
answered as if she read Lennox's very thoughts. "Ahab
gave me a purpose and a sense of belonging. I grew up
hating Christians, hating God. I thought this was a way
to be a part of something bigger than myself."

Easton waited for Lennox to say something,
anything. Silence was all Lennox could produce. She
didn't understand, but wanted to.

Easton nodded and continued, "They were giving me the injections of Venom to turn me when Eli raided the lab I was at. That's where I first met him. He pulled the IVs from my veins, only not in time. My eyes were already wild and my humanity was slowly slipping away from my identity. I can remember feeling a pull from within not to give in to the Venom, then it was lights out. Next thing I remember is waking up in a Sparrow hospital room with my hands and feet fastened to a bed. I know now that they were trying to cure me."

Lennox fumbled around the words Easton said. She had so many questions. There was so much she did not understand. How could someone as beautiful and pure as Easton ever be a Prowler? But Easton wasn't a Prowler anymore. And if Easton could be who she is today, then Sky could be whole again, too. He could be a Sparrow again, someone who brought safety, not danger. Someone who loved, not hated.

"Wait." Lennox sat straighter. "Are you telling me there's a cure for Prowlers?"

"No, it's not that simple." Easton shook her head. "There's no cure, not a scientific one, anyway."

She rested her delicate, tan hands on the table.

"Then how—"

"By faith. *By God.* There's no reasonable earthly explanation, really. I just know Eli and his daughter Cameron… they never gave up on me. They said they saw a spark of goodness in me, which gave them the tiniest ember of hope that I could be saved, set free from the curse of darkness that boiled on the inside of my Prowler veins." She smiled. "And they were right. God can turn the darkest of hearts into a bright pillar of light. You know that, right?"

"Yes." Finally, Lennox understood why Easton had always been so closed off. With a past such as that, she would be too.

Hope ignited in her like a wildfire. If God could cure Easton, He could cure Sky.

She just had to find him. Now, she had evidence he could recover and would never give up.

Chapter 8

It was midnight and Lennox still could not turn off her brain. She lay on a stiff, thin army cot with the feeling her heart was crushed with every beat. Her brain was overloaded and overwhelmed.

With Sparrow City so far away and surrounded by furious Regime soldiers, she now thought of the safety of her canvas tent as "home." She missed Clover, her adopted sister, and Grizz, her German shepherd, but at least she had Oliver nearby. Family and friends truly made a place home.

She held the picture Sky had drawn of her and read the Psalm written at the bottom. "I will say of the Lord, 'He is my refuge and my fortress, my God, in whom I trust.'" That's what she had to do. She had to let God be her refuge. She had to trust. But….

Oh! How she wished to be back in that field with Sky as the fireflies and silver stars twinkled against the dark backdrop of the night sky. If only he was here, safe. She believed from the depths of her soul that Sky still lived and felt certain that her heart would sense it if Sky had… If Sky was….

Lennox couldn't finish the thought, not even to herself. She struggled desperately to see a purpose in a future that did not include him. She, of course, knew there had to be one, but feeling and knowing were two very different things.

Tears rolled down her cheeks onto her flat pillow. It felt as if an ocean of heartbreak lived under her skin. She needed God to hold it all together, to hold *her* all together. "God, please help me understand Your plan. Inside, I'm as lost as Sky is on the outside. I know there's more. I know at the end of it all, You will bring all the pieces together. Give me patience until You do. Give me the strength to wait on Your timing."

Sucking in her breath, she gathered the precious drawing tightly to her chest, near her heart, and held it there until sleep finally swept her away.

God had worked on her heart as she slept, and after only a few hours of rest, Lennox arose slightly groggy, but with purpose. She still had much to live for—to fight for. She felt the assurance that only God could give. When people are lost in the dark, they search for the light. Sky still had to be searching.

As she wiped the sleep from her eyes, she yawned and put on her gray jumpsuit, determined to conquer her doubts, fears, and confusion with hope. She could not see to the end, and she did not fully understand God's exact plan, but she was finished denying His ability or His power. God was in control of her life—now and forever. Just as the walls of Jericho came down in the Bible, so had hers. They crashed down around her all last night.

"I *will* find you, Sky," she whispered to herself, reaffirming her faith and conquering her fears and questions.

Lennox readied herself for another day of facing combatants. She strapped her handgun around her thigh and secured a belt of medical supplies to her waist. Picking up her Stryker and throwing the strap over her shoulder, she walked out of the tent, whispering a simple, but faith-filled prayer. "Lord, let us save as many as we can today. In Jesus' name, amen."

She made her way to the Mess Hall to grab a quick breakfast before her next rescue assignment, not knowing when she'd get her next real meal. She had to eat when there was time to keep her physical strength on the field. She looked up to the morning sky, hoping the sun would hit her face. Instead, blood-red clouds rippled to the east. As days grew darker, the earth became a wretched place, hungry to devour its inhabitants.

In the Mess Hall, Sparrows were packed in like sardines at the few tables and benches provided. Oliver and Easton waved her over. Lennox grabbed a packet labeled "veggie omelet." She could tell it was going to be disgusting by the mushy feel of the package, so she grabbed a water to wash it down before she joined her brother and captain.

"Good Morning." Easton scooted to make room on the bench for her with a smile.

"Morning." Lennox returned the smile and

squeezed in, setting her meal on the table.

Oliver let out a deliberate, slow breath. "We're doing a supply drop in twenty and it would be useful to have a medic. If you—"

"I'm in."

Oliver chuckled a little, his sincere smirk reminding her of when they were kids. "Okay, good. It's good to see you so driven all the time."

She nodded, tapping her fingers on the table as she examined his face. She knew that even though the dark rub of too little rest stained the skin beneath his eyes, Oliver would never admit his exhaustion. He would put forward nothing less than an image of strength—as a leader should. She sighed and turned to Easton. "Any word from Tomas on where Ahab is? Any intel?"

Easton shook her head and licked her lips. "No." She paused and her mouth formed a hard line as she furrowed her brows. "He took a cyanide pill before I even questioned him."

"How is that possible with the serum debilitating him?" Lennox asked.

Oliver rested his elbows on the table and folded

his hands and also looked at Easton.

"I don't know, but when I went in to question him, he was already dead." She cleared her throat and stood, patting Lennox on the shoulder. "I have to talk to Sia and Max. I'll see you both in twenty."

Oliver waved after taking a bite of his own packaged eggs. "Okay, see ya in a few."

Lennox's mind jumped to suspicions as she watched her commander swish through the door. "Oliver, what do you think really happened? You know—" Lennox stopped herself. It was not her place to share Easton's story. She took another bite and sipped her water, forcing the nasty excuse for nutrition down her throat. She put the bottle on the table and picked at her meal by breaking away the eggs one-by-one, lost in her thoughts.

Oliver spoke up. "Easton told me she told you about her past." He placed a hand on the back of his neck and lowered his voice. "About her involvement with the Regime."

"Mm-hmm," she nodded, eyes darting around the Mess Hall to see if anyone overheard. She swallowed another bite of her meal.

"I would have told you, but it wasn't my story to tell." Oliver folded his arms again back on top of the table. "She didn't kill Tomas."

Lennox raised her eyes and shook her head. "I know." Easton would not have killed him. Suicide was the culprit. She refocused. "And I'm not mad at you. I don't blame her for not telling anyone. I understand."

Oliver's tone matched his increase in volume as he relaxed. "So, what do you think? You think Sky's really out there?" Do you believe he can recover from the Venom like Easton if he is?"

"I do." She looked up from her MRE and to her brother. "Do you think I'm crazy?"

"Not one bit. You're my sister. I will always believe with you and stand right beside you. Remember, I already told you that. I know if anyone's testimony could give you impossible faith, it's Easton's."

"Exactly." A surge of fresh energy filled her. "I mean, it was impossible for her, but God still stepped in and saved her. If He did it for her, I know He can do it for Sky. That is, if we can…" Lennox hesitated. *He could be anywhere.* For all they knew, he was a million miles away.

"We'll find him," Oliver said sincerely, lacking all jest.

"We'll find him," Lennox confirmed.

Finishing off the last bite of food, Oliver stood. "Shall we go save the world, now?"

Lennox laughed, the most genuine laugh she'd expelled in a long time. Who would have ever thought she would play any sort of part in saving the world? She stood. "Let's."

Lennox's confidence surged as she arrived at the convoy side-by-side with her brother. To have him there meant more to her than she could express. He had saved thousands of Defier hostages from the Regime's death grip, and today, they were going to save countless more. God was making them conquerors against all odds.

Looking around, Lennox saw the best of the best—Sparrows who were strong, not only in physical stature, but mentally and spiritually as well. Ace, Oliver, Lennox, and Easton made up one rescue team. The other consisted of two large men and a young woman—who was about the same size as Lennox in height and athletic build. They were led by a man named Faraday, whose gladiator muscles and amber, crystal-clear eyes were marked with determination. Lennox was not one to bet, but if she were, she'd bet this mission would be a success by looking at the Sparrows involved.

"All right, listen up!" Easton took charge. "We will approach the safe zone in two directions—from the north and west. Not only have Regime soldiers been spotted, but the new genetically altered mountain lions have as well. The big cats are not to be underestimated. We just got word from Sparrow City that they took out an entire crew not too far from here two weeks ago. They're smart, and instead of traveling alone like normal, they travel in packs, sometimes as many as ten to a dozen at a time." Easton motioned to someone to the far right of her. "Max and Sia insist on spraying each one of us with a deterrent they concocted. From the small amount of information and time they've had to research them, they can give no guarantee it works, however."

Out of the corner of her eye, Lennox saw Sia and Max argue as they walked with two large spraying devices.

"You're going to break it!" Sia huffed.

"No, *you're* going to break it," Max retorted.

Easton sighed and set her mouth into a hard line. "All right, who's first?"

Max lifted up the nozzle of his container and grinned, ear-to-ear, squishing his freckles together.

"Are you serious? Out of all the technology we have, you're going to 'spray,'" Ace threw up air quotes with his fingers, "us with this... what is it... mountain lion repellent? Like insect spray. Like, they're some kind of insect? These things are beasts and you're telling me, that this..." he pointed to the sprayer in Max's hand, "is going to keep them away?" Ace raised his dark eyebrows, which crinkled his onyx skin and widened his deep brown eyes.

"Ah, come on, man. It's better than nothing. I'll go first." Faraday marched forward and nudged Ace out of the way, turning to give him a wink as if to say, "Just appease them, Sparrow."

Ace stepped back and rolled his eyes, "Okay, if you insist. But if this spray doesn't work, you're the first one I'm pushing down." He laughed heartedly.

"You, big chicken," Faraday countered. Max sprayed the mountain lion deterrent on the outer layers of Faraday's jumpsuit. "This stuff reeks."

"Oh, yeah, lots of chemicals," Max said, not cracking a smile.

"Geez, is it even safe to put on us?" Ace chimed in.

"Of course!" Sia furrowed her naturally perfect arched brows. "We would never cause harm to any of you."

"Not on purpose, anyway," Max snorted. It was supposed to be a joke, but he was the only one who laughed.

Sia rolled her eyes, as she usually did when Max tried to be funny. "It should work underneath your Kev disk. The nanotubes don't prevent smells from passing through." Sia waved Sparrows forward for spraying. "It'll work, trust me." A few Sparrows stepped up and allowed the female scientist to spray them with the concoction.

"Next!" Max shuffled through people instead of waiting for them to go to him. Lennox held out her arms and spun, allowing Max to spray the deterrent on her.

After Easton received her "treatment," she said, "The safe zone is located off a ridge of cliffs known as the Texas bluffs. The cliffs are great for protection, but not so great for rescues. We have to be sure to move slow and with purpose. The GWS may be deactivated, but the destruction it has caused is still in effect." She cleared her throat. "And let's not forget, where there are Regime soldiers, there are Prowlers. No sightings of them have been reported yet, but we know they are stealthier and faster than any lone scouts. Do not let them get inside your head. Max and Sia are working on neuro blockers—"

"Yes, yes, that's right!" Max held up his finger and tilted his head as if to say, "Soon."

"We hope to have them ready by your next mission." Sia swallowed hard. She must have understood how important that type of technology was to the Sparrows. "Good luck," she added.

The Sparrows nodded toward the scientists and then Easton gave the order to activate their Kev disks. Lennox pressed the small round disk on her shoulder and watched as bulletproof nanotubes covered her, turning invisible once sealed around her completely.

"All right, let's head out." Oliver took the driver's seat of one Humvee and Faraday took the other.

"See y'all on the other side," Faraday spoke into his com.

Oliver nodded and spoke into his. "Until then."

Chapter 9

Lennox stretched her neck to see the pinnacle of the beautifully striking, uneven earth. A man with a rifle waved from the top. Lennox could not make out his face from the distance, but she could make out his civilian clothes—a red and black plaid shirt and jeans. He stood too close to the edge. Pebbles plummeted down to where the Sparrows stood and the dry, exposed rock appeared as if it could crumble into dust at any minute.

Easton walked around the vehicle and placed her hand over her eyebrows to block the harsh light and falling debris. "No wonder this safe site has remained as untouched by the Regime. With a guard at top to protect the campsite and the questionable access, I can see why the enemy has avoided it until now."

"So, what. We're trekking up that thing?" Ace asked. He rubbed his forehead and clicked his tongue. "I don't know about this. It doesn't look stable enough to climb."

"What, afraid of heights?" Lennox teased. Ace was a go-getter, no matter what the odds appeared to be. "After all you've been through, gunfights... explosions... *this*," Lennox pointed up, "scares you?"

He clicked his tongue to the roof of his mouth again. "No! But, I mean, come on. That cliff does not even look like it can maintain its own weight, let alone ours. What if we climb up and cause too much of a shift and it all comes crashing down, burying us underneath? Being buried alive does not sound fun, and maybe, just maybe, it's one of my phobias."

Easton cleared her throat and gained everyone's attention, ignoring Ace's concern. She had most likely checked with scientists in the first place—or so Lennox hoped—because maybe Ace had a valid point. Easton would not put them in harm's way—not intentionally, anyway, as Max would say.

Faraday and his crew assembled around the front of the Humvee with the others. "We're climbing up the cliff in pairs. The Defiers here have carved out a ledge we can follow all the way to the top, but watch your footing for loose rock. There are men, women, and children depending on us for supplies and protection, so let's not waste any more time on 'what-ifs.'" Faraday squeezed Ace's shoulder. "It'll be fine."

Ace nodded and followed in line with the rest of the crew, gathering equipment to carry up the steep trail. Faraday managed to grab multiple pre-packed sacks of provisions and loaded them on his back. Oliver and Ace did the same. Lennox made sure she had her medical gear and grabbed anything else she could.

"Oliver and I will lead the way and Faraday will take the back," Easton instructed. "Stay close together." She moved toward the narrow hiking path.

Following behind her brother and Easton, Lennox walked alongside Ace. With the first step up on the slanted piece of earth, Lennox already felt the looseness of the ground beneath her. She walked on the outside, close to the ledge so Ace could hug his body near the rock, but walking two-by-two was a struggle, and soon, the path turned narrower.

98

Oliver inched forward, taking the lead with Easton close behind him. Everyone else followed their example. Small particles whooshed out from the ledge with each step. With Ace behind her and Easton in front of her, Lennox trusted her team to catch someone if any should slip.

Clink....

Clink....

Clink....

Larger pebbles crashed into the base and against the tan metal of the Humvees.

Lennox carefully turned and saw Ace's foot slip right along with the falling rocks. "Ace!" Lennox grabbed his arm. "You're okay, just regain your footing," she soothed, noting the panic in his eyes. Her strength strained to support his off-balanced weight.

The troop froze.

Lennox's muscles screamed at her as they strained to support Ace's weight without off-setting her balance. Easton grabbed Lennox's arm to add leverage.

Ace slid his boot back on the path, stabilizing his foot onto the narrow ledge. "Phew. That was a close one. Thanks, Len."

"No problem. You'd do the same for me."

"You know it."

Lennox's heart beat too fast in her chest from the adrenaline rush. All the muscles in her legs tightened and her feet hugged the loose ground through her boots. This high up, not one of them could afford a fall. The nanotubes of the Kev disk could only protect them from so much.

"Everyone okay?" Oliver asked. He waited for each Sparrow to give a thumbs up.

They continued up, curving around the hill and trekking higher and higher until they reached the wide and flat summit of the bluff. Lennox walked to the edge and looked down. The view was breathtaking. A wide canyon filled with dry shrubs and dead cottonwoods stretched between towering bluffs all the way to the horizon. Vertical earth framed the ancient watershed's bed with tan sandstone, casting dark shadows on the flat ground as if to announce their enviable elevation. It was a wilderness larger than Lennox anticipated, and she tried not to imagine what it looked like when it was green. Longing for lost paradise threatened her motivation. She raised her hand as a visor and counted the miles until a burly man in plaid approached.

"I'm glad y'all are here."

Easton pointed to the bags full of food and medicine. "My men have all the supplies you need. At least a couple of months' worth, anyway."

The local man squinted as beams of sunlight washed over his face. "It's not only the supplies we need." He shook his head. "We've spotted a Regime scout along the edge of the cliffs. Not sure how he got all the way up without us seeing him until now."

Oliver took a look around. "We'll find him."

The man shook his head again and his peppered hair fell out-of-place as he rubbed the back of his neck. "Where are my manners? Sorry. I'm Chet." He reached out his hand.

"Oliver." Oliver shook the man's hand. "This is Captain Easton. She's the director of this mission."

Easton stuck out her hand and Chet took it, shaking twice. "Nice to meet you, ma'am."

"Likewise. Where's your camp?"

"Oh, yes! Yes, of course. Camp's that way past the overgrown shrubs to the east, right past the bluff's pond."

Easton shifted her weight and gave a quick nod. "Thank you. I'll have Sparrow Faraday and a few of his men stay here with you to patrol until nightfall and then we'll switch out."

"Why, I appreciate that. We can only spare one man at a time away from the group. The others stand watch around the camp just in case, well, you know why. Even one Regime soldier can be fatal. Oh, and don't get me started on Prowlers." Chet crossed his arms over his chest. "And, did you know they've demonized mountain lions, too? Like we need one more thing to worry about." He cleared his throat, appearing to realize he was rambling. "Anyway... the people at the campsite are expecting you, so you shouldn't have too much trouble with entry once you let them know who you are. Once they see your uniforms, they'll be kind enough to help."

"Of course. Thank you." Easton turned to her men. "Faraday, if you see anything—and I mean *anything*—call in over the com and report."

They all knew one lone man could bring an army behind him.

Chapter 10

The Sparrows followed Easton's cautious lead. On the ride over, in the Humvees, there had been talks of this mission being a trap, so everyone stayed suspicious. Eyes wide and gear ready, Lennox kept her weapon low, but prepared.

The ground on top was different than below. It was moist and the soil on the large bluff sank with every step she took. She wondered how people survived up here for so long. Looking down, she saw the earth in the middle of the bluff was still rich enough to produce, even after all the damage the Global Weather Simulator caused. It was the only way they could have survived solely on the bluff. God had to be intervening.

They paused by the crystal blue pond. Lennox

had never seen such a large watering hole on a bluff-top. It was stunningly beautiful, as if God had dipped His finger in the land and filled it with life, which He may very well have. He provided for the Defiers to give them hope, just as He had to her and Sky with the aurora. No matter how rough it got, she was determined to not allow herself to forget God's provision. He was good, even now.

Easton marched them toward the camp. Soon, they heard voices. They were close. Easton held up a fist. "Slow," she said, waving the Sparrows forward.

Two men popped their heads up from a camouflaged foxhole about twenty feet away. The youngest of the two—who was possibly not even an adult, yet—climbed out and then bent down to help the other—a man who looked as ancient as days.

The Sparrows cautiously moved closer.

"Hey, we've been expecting you," said the older man. Half his teeth were missing and his clothes were tattered. He waved before he stuck out a wrinkled hand to Easton. "Frankie."

"Easton." She dipped her head. "Nice to meet you."

104

"This here," Frankie patted the young man on the chest with a brittle hand, "is my grandson, Martin."

Martin raised a pointer finger to his forehead and tipped his head as if he had a cowboy hat on. "Ma'am." His voice cracked from immaturity.

Easton nodded. "Nice to meet you both. Do you think you can point us in the right direction so we can set up?"

Frankie clicked his tongue. "Right beyond that brush is the main campsite. We tried to keep it compact and keep everyone close and safe."

Easton smiled. "Thank you. Keep up the good work out here."

"Will do!" Frankie placed his hands on his thin waist. "Alright, Martin. Back in the foxhole we go."

Martin gently helped his grandfather in first and then hopped down beside him.

Lennox whispered to Oliver. "How old do you think that boy is?"

"Hard to say." Oliver shook his head. "Thirteen, fourteen?"

The sounds of civilization grew. As men, women, and children came in to view, Lennox and the other Sparrows lowered their weapons, allowing them to hang from the straps.

Children with dirty faces stood in a circle, kicking a soccer ball. Women with sweat on their brow worked in a garden. The only real sign of a raging war were the men who guarded the perimeter of this little oasis with rifles strapped to their backs. Life on the hill seemed peaceful—easy, even—but everyone's clothes and dirt-ridden faces said different. The bluff's inhabitants glanced their way at most, as if they expected them.

A tall man wearing jeans and a shredded shirt approached. "This way," he motioned. He led them to an open space right outside the main living area of the people. "Y'all can set up here. I'm Anthony. I guess you could say I'm in charge of the bluffs. Never wanted to be, though," he sighed. "Anyway, just holler out if you need anything. I've got to get back on guard. Ever since they spotted that wretched Regime scout, everyone has been on edge." With that, he walked away with his rifle on his shoulder.

Easton responded by sizing him up. She did that from time to time though—read people—evaluated them on her own terms. Lennox watched her do it countless times, especially with new acquaintances, just like she had done to her when they first met. She wondered what Easton thought of Anthony because she had no idea what to think of him. He wasn't very friendly, and "did not even want the job," but she respected him for his commitment to protect the people. At least, she liked that he gave the impression he protected them, regardless of his not wanting to. She could see why the people of the bluff chose him. He had every physical attribute of a leader—strong, broad shoulders, towering height, serious eyes, and an authoritative voice. Why didn't he want the role of leader? Maybe the responsibility? The constant worry? She could not blame him for not wanting the position.

Easton scoured the grounds. "Okay, let's set up the tent here with the equipment Max and Sia gave us. We should be able to, at the very least, set up the heat sensor by tonight to track any movement along the cliffs, maybe even the base of it."

A collective "Yes ma'am" was spoken and the Sparrows immediately got to work.

Lennox teamed up with Oliver to unpack the

equipment as the others worked on setting up the tent that would serve as the outpost while they were here.

For now, *this* would be home.

Chapter 11

Night fell over the Texas bluffs. Flickering campfires provided ambient light as every civilian woman and child slept inside tiny dwellings. A dozen civilian men or so paced tirelessly, patrolling the little elevated town.

As Lennox sat near the flames, another group of campground soldiers walked the perimeter of the camp. They were much smaller than their cohorts—not children, not yet adults. They had quivers of arrows strapped to their backs and bows in their hands. They kept watch just as seriously as the grown men. One in particular caught Lennox's eye. She was a teenage girl whose long, fiery red hair and delicate ivory face peeked out from under a black hood.

"Hey, Len!" Oliver called as he headed her

way. "You ready?"

She did a final check on her uniform and gear. "Ready."

As she walked with her brother and left the locals to their posts, Lennox took in the blackness. She had never seen the distance so dark. Tiny embers from the orange flames behind her floated on the gentle breeze.

Lennox turned on the light of her helmet and adjusted her night-vision goggles. She would need them while away from the campfire and when she was forced to turn off her headlamp. "How long do you think before we will find the scout?" Lennox asked as the dim light from her helmet shone on Oliver's face.

"Not sure, but I hope soon. They've got a good thing going here. I'd hate to see another safe site lost." The corners of his mouth curved downward. "Well, as safe as you can get now days."

"Do you think the enemy scout already transmitted this location?" Lennox swallowed hard, turning off her light and placing the goggles over her eyes. The darkness of night turned to what looked like a green-lit day.

"Nah, they don't work like that. Our spies have verified that Scouts remain dark. No tech, no communication. That's one reason they're so hard to track. They leave no twenty-first century trail."

"Well, at least we know they won't be dropping bombs on us yet."

"Yeah." Oliver's chuckle was a little pained. "I guess there's always a bright side."

As they walked, she clearly saw every stick on the ground and the scattered trees ahead. The pond glistened green. If it weren't for the goggles, Lennox would have walked right into the water.

Frankie and Martin waved from the foxhole as Lennox and Oliver walked by. They looked like little green aliens with bug eyes. Ah... goggles. Sparrow scientists had provided extra supplies for civilian use. Easton would have made sure they received them right away. Lennox supposed she and Oliver looked a little like aliens, too.

When they picked up their pace, it did not take long to reach the men standing guard near the bluff's cliff alongside Faraday and his Sparrow team. Even through the night-vision goggles, Lennox could tell the civilian guards were dog-tired. She wondered how long had they been patrolling and when they last got a good night's rest. Her heart ached for their fatigue. In contrast, Faraday and the other Sparrows looked like they could go another round if needed. She wasn't surprised.

Faraday lifted his chin in greeting. "Oliver. Lennox."

"All quiet?" Oliver asked. "Any movement?"

"Nope, not a thing. We'll get him, though. He has to try to get back to the Regime sometime, and when he does, we'll intercept him."

Faraday had the confidence Lennox envied, but his surety helped her believe they'd find the Regime scout before he caused too much damage.

"You still need us here, or should we head to the camp?" Faraday asked.

Oliver shook his head. "We've got plenty reinforcements. Take the local guards with you. While your team watches the camp, those guys can get some sleep."

"These guys sure could use some solid rest," Faraday nodded. "On it." Reaching for his com,

Faraday spoke to his team, "Time to move out."

"Len, cover far west. I'll stay at the main access point."

"Got it." Lennox took her position.

The cliff's edge looked like a mere wrinkle in the earth. Lennox gave thanks for good depth perception. as she did not want to let her foot get too close to the edge. She already had her fair share of tumbling down rock. With the closest Sparrow stationed over half a mile away, she paced, scanning left and right to try to cover her entire area. Behind her, the land got lost in brush and small trees. She'd have to run her heat sensor to detect any movement along that way.

One hour passed.

Nothing.

Another hour.

Nothing.

At the third hour mark near the edge of the brush, her goggles picked up a thermal reading. She caught her breath and her heart stopped.

It could be nothing. Lord, please let it be nothing.

She chastised herself for the cowardly prayer. Of course she wanted it to be something. That was the whole reason she was out here. She wanted to catch the Regime scout, so she made a new request.

Lord, if it is the scout, let us capture him without anyone dying.

She pressed her com. "I've got a heat signature along the brush on the far west side." Readying her weapon, she inched closer.

"Copy. I'm headed your way." Oliver's voice came through, giving her comfort just from the sound of it. If anyone would have her back she'd want it to be him. He always protected her. If he ran, he could make it to her in a few minutes. Should she wait?

No. I can do this. God, I can do this because You are with me.

She could not risk losing the target. Lennox advanced toward the masculine figure as questions invaded her mind. Did he see her coming? Did he have a heat censor too? Did he see her as she saw him? With each step closer, the unidentified man or animal seemed to move that much farther away.

Not again.

Lennox let out steady breaths. Everything was green except for the red and yellow figure that eluded her. She pressed her com again. "I can't seem to even get close to it."

She waited for a response.

A minute passed.

"Do you copy?"

The silence caused more adrenaline to rush through her veins. Her heart thudded against her ribcage.

"Oliver?"

She stopped in her tracks. A man's frame stood right in front of her, causing her heat sensor to show only red. Taken off guard, she gasped and took a step back while firing a clumsy shot into a tree. Frustrated, she fired again and again, but each time the figure dodged the blue-serum bullet. She inhaled, took aim, and fired. She released her breath, sure it was a clear shot. The figure moved like the speed of light, too quick for anything or anyone to hit. It was faster than any physical move she could do.

Huh? Enough with these guys!

Lennox inhaled again, forcing herself to align

with her target once more. She fired.

Miss.

Again.

Are you kidding me?

It seemed as if the scout taunted her, begging her to try again. What kind of freak of nature was this guy?

Then, out of the darkness, hands crushed around Lennox and her tech. The nanotubes did not feel as if they could hold up to the amount of pressure he enforced. Her Stryker hung off her body like a mere accessory. Her feet dangled in the air. She kicked and squirmed as much as she could under the man's bone-crushing strength and then....

"Get. Out. Of. My. Head."

"What?" The figure's grip loosened until it released Lennox, and then chaotically bounced from one place to the next.

Lennox saw the animal-like movements in the man now. She stood confused and reached for her weapon. She followed the scout with her gun, trying to get a clean shot.

"Sky!" the scout screamed, his expression

shifting to a mask of torture as he held his hands against his temples. "Get out! Get out of my head, Sky!"

Chapter 12

Lennox froze. The name hit her like a bucket of ice.

Sky.

The Regime scout said, "Sky."

Didn't he?

She shook her head and blinked. *I can't be going crazy. Not now! Lord, help me to be strong. Let me not be distracted.*

The scout crouched low to the ground with its head in its hands, making sounds that crossed between mumbling, cursing, and weeping. It barely moved, but for a slight rocking back and forth. Lennox lifted her weapon and fired one shot.

Hit!

The Sparrow serum capsule met its target and the Regime scout crumpled to the ground.

"Lennox! Come in! Are you okay?"

"Oliver!" *Thank God.* "I'm near the brush along the west side, about forty feet from the clearing." Her shoulders rose and fell with every breath she took. "We have him! I got the scout!"

Lennox heard her brother's footsteps running toward her.

As soon as Oliver reached her side, he slapped her back. "Great job, Len!"

"Thanks, but I did not get this one on my own."

"So humble," Oliver said, patting his sister on the shoulder. "I know God had your back! He always has and always will!"

"Yeah, but that's not..." *what I meant.* But there was no time to truly explain.

Oliver moved straight to the scout. Picking up the man from the ground, Oliver said, "Man, he's a big guy, isn't he?"

"I think he's a type of Prowler." Flashes of the man bouncing back and forth to avoid her shots replayed in her head.

"Really? Why?" Oliver had the scout upright and cuffed.

119

"Just the way he moved. I mean, one minute he was right in front of me, and then the next, to the left, and then to the right. He's impossibly fast. Like…." Lennox trailed off, lost in thought. She wanted to ask the scout a few of her own questions. Was Sky with him? Here? Now?

"Like the other Prowlers?"

"Yeah, but smarter. And maybe even stronger. He did not even try to take over my mind. It was like he was playing a game with me, taunting me, luring me closer for—" She shook her head. "For his own entertainment."

"Odd. We'll question him back at the campsite and figure out what's going on. He'll talk."

"I hope so."

"Target secure." Oliver spoke into his com. "We're heading back to camp now. Stay alert, there could be more headed our way."

A collective chime of "Yes sir" came in through Lennox's ear piece.

Lennox walked beside her brother and behind the Regime scout he prodded forward. As they neared the foxhole, Frankie and Martin stuck their heads up.

"You got him! You got him!" Martin sprang out of the foxhole and ran forward, giving Lennox a high five. "I knew y'all would get him! Man... I've never seen such a thing. Why are his veins glowing blue?" Martin approached the scout, not showing an ounce of fear.

Lennox moved between him and the Regime scout. "That's the Sparrow serum the scientists created. God gave them the idea for it. Pretty cool, huh?"

"Cool? It's spectacular! Hey, Grandpa, you seeing this?" Martin walked alongside Lennox as they continued.

"Yeeaahh, I see it all right!" Frankie yelled from the foxhole. "That is something else, ain't it?"

As they passed, the Regime scout started to jerk. His steps became clunky like a zombie's.

"Whoa." Martin backed off a little.

"Martin, you stay here with your grandfather and keep watch. It's very important to stay on guard, as usual." Oliver held the now-convulsing scout with both hands to support his weight.

"Yes sir!" Martin jumped in the foxhole beside his grandfather and saluted.

"We'll be here," Frankie reassured.

The campfire provided a glaring glow in Lennox's goggles. She removed them and Oliver did the same.

Men on guard rushed forward. The scout growled as Easton came into view.

"Let's get him to the Sparrow tent to see if we can get anything out of him," she commanded.

"Yes ma'am." Lennox nodded and walked toward the tent as Oliver followed close behind.

This man had to know something about Sky, about where he was and if he was okay. She hoped Easton would give her permission to ask him a few questions of her own, because she was sure he knew something that could lead her to the truth.

As they walked by the fire, the scout hissed as if he was burned by it. A shudder moved through Lennox's frame, recalling how the Regime and Thompson forced her to stick the branding iron in the flames... how they made branding her like an animal a game. She shivered again and forced the memory to the back of her mind as she pulled the Sparrow tent flap wide for Oliver and the scout to get through.

After being in the dark for so long, the lights inside the tent were almost blinding. It took a few moments for Lennox's pupils to adjust. Oliver sat the prisoner on a cot.

Easton came in and stared at him with her hands on her hips.

"What is it?" Oliver asked.

Did Eason know this man, too? If so, given her past connection to the Regime, how many more did Easton know or have ties to?

Captain Easton glowered at the scout. "His name is Rayyan. This man helped me when I was held by the Regime. He told me not to volunteer to become a Prowler. He fought for me, and now…." She trailed off.

Oliver reached out and squeezed her shoulder. "I'm sorry."

"It's okay. I had hoped he'd gotten out." Easton's jaw flexed. "Like me."

"Is he a Prowler?" Lennox asked.

"His eyes don't glow." Easton's eyebrows scrunched together. "That's usually the tell. Why do you ask?"

"Lennox says he moved like one, with impossibly fast agility," Oliver spoke for her.

"Oh." Easton sighed heavily, disappointed all over again. "Did he try to get inside your head?"

"No, but the Regime is modifying their scouts, right? Keeping their full mental functions but altering their physical abilities? They're...." Lennox sucked in a breath as a cold wave of truth rushed over her. "They're perfecting the Venom."

"If he's a Prowler, I'd say yes." Easton nodded. "And if that's the case, more cities will be in danger sooner than later." Her eyes wandered from Lennox to Oliver. "I'll take care of him and make sure he will be ready for questioning by morning."

Lennox cleared her throat. Did she really want to bring up what she heard the scout say in the brush? She bit her lip. Yes. She had to. "Umm... Easton? There's something else you should know."

"What?"

"While we were fighting, he had me in his grasp and then...." Lennox paced, rubbing her forehead.

"And then *what*, Lennox?" Oliver pressed.

"It's going to sound crazy." Lennox sighed,

gathering the words she needed to say. "He let me go, and as he did, he yelled for *Sky* to get out of his head."

Easton's expression mirrored Oliver's, who had one eyebrow arched toward his hairline.

"I know it's crazy, and I know I have had false alarms before, but this time is different. I know what I heard."

"Are you sure?" Easton asked.

"Positive." Her pulse slammed in her neck. There. It was out there. Lennox did not have to keep it to herself any more. The scout's words were all the proof Lennox needed. "Sky is alive."

And close.

Chapter 13

After going over her encounter with the scout more times than she could count, Lennox was too keyed up by the debriefing to sleep. Oliver's and Easton's questions—and later words of comfort—jumbled in her brain. They agreed that Sky was most likely alive and nearby, but also warned her of the odds of actually rescuing him. He was possibly able to take control of Rayyan's thoughts. Did it mean Sky fought the Venom in his veins? Fought for faith? Was fighting for… her? It had to.

But where was he now? Easton said she'd ask about Sky in the morning, during questioning. But could a Regime scout be trusted to answer truthfully?

Lennox lay on her cot, staring at empty space.

Everyone close to her was sound asleep. She prayed, silently, knowing the Lord heard the thoughts of her heart.

Lord, I'm going to trust You with Sky as I said I would. Thank You for giving me the answer of whether or not he is really alive. I'm going to keep fighting. Please give me the strength and wisdom to do so. In Jesus' name, amen.

Lennox closed her eyes. Soothed by the gentle breathing of her comrades and the quiet confidence of knowing her prayer was heard, she drifted to sleep.

Slam!

A hand crashed over her mouth. Before her sleepy mind could react, Lennox was yanked from her cot and was outside in a flash. She kicked and elbowed her captor, but her movements were useless flails against his massive strength.

She glimpsed the men who stood guard out of the corner of her eye, but for all her struggling, her captor's steps were silent and his hand remained clamped over her lips. The guards' lack of reaction demonstrated they did not see or hear her.

The hand loosened just enough for Lennox to

open her mouth and chomp the top portion of the intruder's hand.

"Ow!" the man hissed. He added pressure to her mouth and ran until they were surrounded by brush and young trees. When he stopped, he set her feet gently on the ground, but kept a firm hold with her back pressed against him. His breath tickled her ear. "Lennox. Don't scream, okay?"

Her heart pounded so hard she thought it would break her ribs. *That voice.*

"It's okay, Lennox. It's me."

She gasped. Could it really be…?

His grip loosened enough so she could turn in his arms. She tilted her face up and blinked.

"It's me." He nodded. "It's really me."

She was unable to grasp what she saw, but she'd know that voice anywhere.

"Sky!" She wrapped her arms around him, breathing in his earthy scent. She had so many questions, but her words failed and she could not function enough to say anything, let alone, a complete, coherent sentence. His arms tightened in the tenderest embrace, and when her feet left the ground this time, she did not protest.

"Oh, how I've missed you," Sky said, placing a sweet kiss on her forehead.

"You have no idea." Now she wanted answers that only he could give. "Where have you—? What did they—? How did you—?" Her words tumbled out in unfinished phrases. She could not pick one to ask first, so she gave up and melted into the strength of his arms, instead.

Sky. Here. Holding her.

His embrace brought so much relief it was as if a thousand pounds were lifted from her shoulders. For the first time since he was taken from her, she truly breathed again... felt again.

Sky loosened his arms from around her, found her hand, and laced his fingers through hers. "Here, sit down."

Sky guided her until she sat on a large, cool rock and then lowered himself close beside her.

"I can see in the dark pretty well, now." His tone said he wanted to laugh, but he didn't. "I'm sorry it took so long to get to you. I've been following you for a while, trying to protect you. I did not have the opportunity to get you by yourself." At this, he did chuckle drily. "I didn't think the other Sparrows would take a Prowler coming into their camp lightly, or even understand it. I'm not so sure they'll forgive me or... if *you* have forgiven me."

The soft glow of the moon gave just enough light for Lennox to see his shoulders droop. She shook her head, noticing his eyes only glowed like a Prowler's along the outer rim of his irises. "There's nothing to forgive. Sky, nothing's changed."

He shook his head. "Everything's changed. *I've changed.* I-I've done terrible things that I can never take back." He closed his eyes and took a deep breath.

"We all have fallen short, Sky, not just you. And it wasn't really you. It was the Venom."

She squeezed his hand tighter. Her Sky was back. She had prayed so long for this moment, but now that it was here, she hardly believed it was real.

"Hmph. Yeah, the Venom." He tensed. "Lennox, the Venom will always be inside of me. It will always course through me and be a voice inside my head."

"But you've found a way to fight against it!

130

Your faith in God is greater." Lennox would not back down, and she would not let Sky give up.

"I want it to be, but you don't understand. It's like walking through quicksand. The more I fight against the darkness inside of me, the more it fights back."

"There's darkness in each one of us, but we don't have to fear the darkness when we walk in the light." She believed it and often repeated that phrase to other Sparrows. "Sky, you can beat this. God will give you the strength to do it. I know He will. Look how far He's brought you. You were a full-fledged Prowler and now look at you. You're... you!"

Sky shook his head. "For now, anyway."

She thought back to how he carried her out of the crumbling building, only to turn into a Prowler a few minutes later. She understood what He said. She traced the outline of the *D* on her arm with her forefinger. "This time's different."

"How do you know that for sure? I've been to hell's gates and back. The darkness whispers to me." He cleared his throat. "I'll stay hidden, but just promise me, Lennox. Promise you'll end it if I ever try to hurt you. Just shoot me and get it over with, okay?

"What?" A lump formed in her throat. "No." She sat up straighter. "No, I won't just shoot you… and no, it's not okay you stay hidden. Others need to know you're alive and not a Prowler anymore. And maybe it's time we all push back a little harder against the darkness."

She had not had this much fiery faith boil inside her since the very first time she stood against the Regime. How could she not? God brought Sky back!

"This—*you*—you are a living testimony of the power of God, and as much as I love you and want you to be comfortable, you can't stay hidden." Boldness rose within her like she'd never felt before. Lennox released Sky's hand and stood. "It's time we take back what the enemy has stolen."

Sky stood, facing her. "I figured you'd say something like that. Just… please. Say you will do what's necessary to protect others from me. I don't want to hurt anyone else, especially you, but I had to see, *to know*, that you were okay." He pulled her in closer. "I'll stay out of sight, but I'll be close, okay?"

"What? What does that even mean?" Lennox

stared into his eyes, waiting, but as she watched, the outer edge of his frame fizzled away as if he dissolved before her. "Sky?" Her eyes remained on him, confused and bewildered. "No. Sky, no!"

And then he was gone, vanishing into the night with no part of him left. No evidence that he had been there at all.

Lennox's hand grasped air. Sky was just... gone.

As the orange moon receded into the pitch-black sky, darkness encompassed her. It fell around her and went through her. She turned to find her love, but as she did, the canvas of her cot met her skin.

Her eyes flew open.

She lay on her bed, sweating through her Sparrow tights.

A dream.

Was it all a dream?

Impossible!

She sat up, wanting to scream. *How could something so real be just a dream?* She was beginning to hate her dreams. Even the good ones. They brought too much pain when she awoke.

Chapter 14

Lennox wiped the tears that streamed down her face and wondered how her subconscious could be so cruel to her soul. With an ache in every part of her, she arose from her cot.

Clink.

She looked down to where the noise came from and lost her breath. She gasped. On the ground was a small, shiny piece of gold that was melted on one side, but still in the shape of a heart. The back of her mother's locket... the one she had disabled the Global Weather Simulator with... the one she lost after Sky carried her out of the burning building.

She reached down and picked it up, rubbing her thumb over the metal. The engraved words partially remained. *We walk by faith, not by sight.* Except the word "sight" was burned off, leaving only the first letter.

Sky *was* here. It wasn't just a dream. But where did he go and why did he leave her here?

She could not answer any of the questions that rumbled in her head. All she knew was that her heart hurt more than anything she had ever felt before, even more than the scar on her chest from when the Regime bombed her prom.

Sky, where are you?

Lennox took in a deep breath and held the piece of locket tightly in her fist. All of her fellow Sparrows still slept peacefully—except the ones on watch, of course. She forced herself to get ready, tucking the remnants of her dream in her jumpsuit pocket and quietly exited the Sparrow tent.

She inhaled the fresh air provided by the seclusion of the bluffs. The night's moon still hung in darkness, reflecting the light of the sliver of sun that was just coming over the cliffs. Low pockets of fog swept the ground and the humidity made breathing laborious.

Lennox thought about how nice it was to not wear the full tech suit and face-mask all the time like she had to when the Global Weather Simulator was still active, but the atmosphere still seemed menacing. How much longer would the earth hold itself together? Only God really held it together now. For how long, she did not know.

She sat on a tree stump near the fire pit. Embers were all that was left. Beautiful specs of orange flickered against gray ash. She reached in her pocket and brought out the broken locket. Her eyes roamed, hoping to find clues that Sky might have left behind—clues that would take her to him.

"Mornin', Lennox."

The southern twang gave the voice away. Lennox knew it had to be Ace even without turning around to see him. "Morning, Ace." She wrapped her hands around her legs and rested her head on top of her knees, making herself small. She hid her mother's locket in her palm.

Ace found a stump and sat next to her. "How'd you sleep last night?"

She couldn't share her dream with anyone else

136

when she still tried to process the pain of it herself. "Fine, thanks." She swallowed hard around the truth. "You?"

"Good, except for all the mumbling you did that woke me up." Ace rested his muscular forearms on the top of his thighs and popped his knuckles.

Lennox felt the heat flush her cheeks. "Oh, I'm so sorry." She squeezed her arms tighter around her legs. "I hope I did not bother anyone else." *I hope I did not embarrass myself.*

He smirked and shook his head. "Don't worry about it. I'm used to it. We all are. There's always one of us that does it at least once a night. Yours sounded serious, though." Ace grabbed a twig and broke it into tiny pieces, throwing them down as he did. "You want to talk about it?"

"Um, no, I'm okay, thanks though." Lennox bit her bottom lip to keep from crying in front of her fellow Sparrow. She had to remain strong, but then thought about it more. She *had* to tell someone. Why not Ace? She cleared her throat. "Actually, there is something." She glanced his way.

He rested his forearms on top of his thighs and

twisted a thin, wiry twig between his fingers. "I'm listening."

Lennox held out her palm and unwrapped her fingers from the piece of jewelry. "I found this on the floor this morning."

His eyes went from the locket to her eyes. "Is that what I think it is?"

"It's a piece of my mother's locket… the one that held the tech my father created. It's the one that brought down and was left at the Regime's main frame."

Ace's jaw dropped. "How in the world…?"

"Last night, I had the most vivid dream of Sky. But now," she fiddled with the locket, "now I don't think it was a dream at all. I think Sky's alive and I think he's here." Lennox raised her brows and waited for Ace to respond.

"Len, you know how crazy that sounds?"

"How else would you explain it?"

Ace shook his head. "I can't, but—"

"Don't tell anyone, please? They'll think I'm crazy." Lennox tucked the locket back in her pocket as fellow Sparrows walked by.

"I won't, I promise," Ace reassured.

A few more seconds passed and the bluff community started to come to life. Children exited their tents along with their mothers and the men on watch nodded to assure them it was clear.

Ace stood and rubbed his hands together, dusting off the remnants of the twig he obliterated. "I'll be right back. Just have to get my gear. Wait for me before you head out and I'll escort you to your position, okay?"

Lennox wanted to laugh. She did not need an escort, not like before. She was a soldier now, too, but Ace still upheld gentlemanly practices with her. Maybe it was because he was the one to pull her away from Sky and onto the Sparrow stealth jet when the building exploded. She'd forgiven him for that already. He'd only been trying to protect her. She understood that now.

"Okay." She managed a smile and stared down, watching the fog as it drifted around her ankles. As Ace saw to his gear, Lennox embraced her quietness.

One of the younger local guards—the red-haired girl—approached, taking Ace's spot. She pulled at a fingernail as if she built up courage. Finally, she turned. "Hey." She offered her hand to Lennox. "I'm Elise."

Lennox shook the girl's thin hand. "Lennox. Nice to meet you."

Elise's eyes were that brilliant shade of green that God seemed to only grant to redheads. Her porcelain skin was dotted with tiny freckles that ran a path across her nose. Elise reminded Lennox of a prettier, female version of Max.

"I noticed you keeping guard the other day. Are you a leader in that group?" Lennox asked because when she saw Elise for the first time, she pointed everyone into position.

"Yeah, I try to be, since I'm the oldest."

"How old are you anyway?"

"Just turned sixteen."

"You any good with that bow?" Lennox nodded to the arrows and bow strapped to Elise's back.

Elise ran a gentle index finger over the feathers on her handmade arrows. "Good enough. They save all the guns for the men, so me and the boys have gotten to be pretty good shots with these." She stared at her quiver and then tilted her head toward Lennox. "Enough to bring home food and stuff, anyway." She smiled.

"Impressive." Lennox returned the smile.

BANG!

That's strange. Lennox tilted her head to the direction of the distant sound. "Was that a gunshot?" she asked. She had been warned the men would have target practice close by.

Elise peered over her shoulder in the direction of the noise. "I think so."

An uneasy feeling stirred in Lennox's gut. She waited, but didn't see or hear anything more than the one shot. "Target practice?"

"Probably." Elise nodded. "Sometimes the guys—"

POP!

BANG!

Lennox and Elise bolted to their feet, drawing their weapons. They looked at each other and then back to where the sound came from. As the shots echoed and bounced off the surrounding cliffs and bluffs, Ace and the rest of the Sparrows rushed out from the tent.

Chaos.

Children ran back to their tents, urged by frantic mothers close on their heels. Lennox took a protective stance in front of Elise.

"Huge mountain lions, at least a dozen of them! Closing in!" one man yelled over his shoulder.

She glanced at Elise. "Nock your arrow. Now!"

They were close and there was no telling the kind of damage these beasts could cause with the Regime's Venom running through their systems.

Movement caught her peripheral vision—a flash of golden brown fur.

"Lion! My nine o'clock!" she shouted. "Be ready!" She tried to track the beast's movement, but it was fast. Too fast, like the man in the woods last night.

One of the creatures pounced onto one of the shooters from behind some bushes to her left. Lennox took aim, firing her weapon once... twice... three times before the mountain lion noticed. When it finally collapsed, an arrow protruded from its hide. Elise had made contact too.

Lennox tossed Elise a smile. "Good shot." She gestured toward the man the lion attacked. "Will you give me a hand with him?"

"You bet."

They ran toward him, his head and torso covered beneath that heavy mound of bloody fur.

"On three, we're going to roll him." Lennox counted off, and with a great heave, they freed the man. "Are you okay, Sir?"

His shirt was ripped from the lion's claws and his face had minor puncture wounds, but none of them looked serious. "I-I'm…." The man's eyes were wide and held the sort of terror Lennox had grown too accustomed to seeing. "I'm fine. I think."

Lennox helped him to a sitting position.

Blood curdling screams came from the tents and Lennox's attention shifted. She threw her sights on the women and children.

"Go," he said. "I'll be fine. Go!"

"I'll stay with him," Elise offered. "Go!"

Lennox ran toward the tents and as she did, her gaze caught movement in the space between them. Farther out from camp, one beast fought against… *another beast?* She squinted, but they moved so fast she couldn't be sure at this distance. She reached for her binoculars.

No, it wasn't two mountain lions. It was a genetically altered lion versus...versus... *A Prowler*—a genetically altered man.

"Prowler!" Lennox shouted, earning the attention of four other Sparrows. "Follow me!"

She stashed her binoculars as she ran and had her weapon ready. The lion rose to its hind legs and crashed its front paws on the shoulders of the Prowler, who grabbed the animal by its neck.

Thrashing. Blood. Saliva. Who would win this battle?

"What are you waiting for?" one man shouted. "Take the shot!".

"But it's fighting the lion for us!" Someone protested on the Prowler's behalf.

"Yeah, and then it will turn on us! It's a mindless Prowler!"

Lennox watched the Prowler as he moved. All she saw was his backside, twisting and turning in full-fledged fight mode.

BANG! BANG! BANG!

The mountain lion fell to the dirt.

The Prowler turned to the crowd that now gathered—men, boys with guns and boys with bows. A fourteen-year-old looked uncertain. His hands shook nervously and sweat dripped from his brow and into his eyes. The boy blinked away the salty fluid and drew the bowstring back, aiming his arrow. It wouldn't be a clean shot if he fired and the Prowler had to sense that, but he lifted his hands in surrender and took a step back.

Surrender? That was not a normal Prowler trait. Most were of the belief that such a response had been stripped from their DNA.

Instinctively, Lennox ran to get a better look at him.

Bloodstained clothes, scratched face, and green eyes that glowed on their outer edges.

Sky.

It's Sky! Her heart pounded like a jackhammer.

She ran to her long-lost friend—the love of her life—wanting to throw herself at him. She missed everything about him and now here he was, with her, in the flesh. But she could not get to him in time.

Five streams of blue laser-lights rested on his

chest with another right between his eyes, a perfect dot marking the kill shot. Steady Sparrow hands waited for the command to open fire. Out of the corner of her eye, another boy lifted his bow and arrow, followed by another. Lennox knew *they* would not wait for an order.

Their hands shook, unsure and unsteady. They barely kept proper aim at their target, but if they fired, there was a chance one of their arrows would go into the Prowler's chest.

Sky's chest.

"No!" Lennox screamed. "Wait!"

Before she could step in front of the already bloody Prowler, the two boys released their arrows.

The projectiles whistled passed her. Sky caught one with his hand and stopped it from piercing his flesh, but the other plowed through his upper right shoulder, causing him to break the other arrow in two. He threw it to the ground and broke the other in half to pull it out in two pieces. He lifted his head and scrunched his face together as he slowly slid the splintered, handmade shaft from one side of his shoulder. Groaning, he reached over to pull out the rest from behind, avoiding reentrance of the tip of the arrow

146

through his flesh.

"Sky!" Lennox threw her body in front of him and held him.

Blood and tears dripped down the back of Lennox's neck. Sky rested his head on her shoulder, his beard tickling her cheek as he melted into her embrace. She soaked him in, every part of him.

It *was* him, really him, here in her arms.

Disbelief overtook her as she closed her eyes and held him tighter, taking everything in. His arms wrapped around her waist. *Ah, Sky.* Hazy voices muddled together. Nothing else mattered except this moment.

Then he let go and softly pushed her away.

"Sky?" She stared at him, puzzled. The angry mob surrounding them came back to life through her senses.

A pair of men pulled Lennox out of the way.

"No!" Lennox fought to get back to him. "His name is Sky. He's not dangerous!"

The arms holding her back were too strong to make headway against, but that did not stop Lennox from digging her feet in the dirt and pushing in his direction.

"Sky, you have to run! They'll kill you!"

Sky stood stoically as the angry mob surrounded him. They didn't know Sky from before. They wouldn't see him as anything other than a Prowler. They couldn't know.

"Get down! Get down!" Men ordered and pointed their weapons, moving closer, taking aim directly at Sky's skull.

Sky crashed to his knees, lifting his hands in surrender. His eyes closed and his head hung defeated. The sleeve of his black uniform was torn where the Regime emblem should have been.

The Regime had changed him, yes. He was a Prowler. But he was not *their* Prowler. In any form, by any alteration of Venom, the Regime could not destroy the man of God within.

He was real. This was not a figment of her imagination or a dream. Sky was here. Tangible. True. And Sky was still Sky. Everything he had just done screamed the old Sky. The man she loved. The one she adored.

Lennox wrestled against the men's grasp and

finally broke one arm free, but was swiftly restricted again. "Stop!" she yelled as loud as her lungs would shout, still fighting with everything in her to get closer to him.

Her fellow Sparrows, the men with rifles, and boys with arrows held their weapons high.

"Can't you see he surrendered?" she pleaded with them. "You must see he's different. Ask Captain Easton. Ask Oliver." *Where are they?* She desperately wished her brother and Captain were here to diffuse the misunderstanding.

The crowd of armed men protested louder. "It's a Prowler, they don't surrender."

"Yeah, he's probably waiting to get inside each one of our heads and turn us against each other."

"He's probably the one who brought the mountain lions here in the first place!"

"We can't let another Prowler in here to rip apart our families! He'll kill us all!"

"No!" she cried. "Not this one. He's different. I *know* him!" Lennox's heart chased the deep ache in her soul. She had never felt more helpless. *Oh God, they're going to kill him. Lord, please give me the strength to get to him. I can't lose him again.* And with that simple prayer, Lennox gave one more, soul-deep jerk against her captors.

She was free. To get to him, they were going to have to go through her first. She wasn't going to lose him again, not ever.

With a quick, "Thank you, Jesus!" she bolted to Sky, raising her hands. "Please! Just hear me out."

Anthony finally walked up to her, rifle in hand. "Darlin', I don't know who you think he is, but he is not who you used to know. Move out of the way."

Lennox planted her feet and kept her hands out in front of her. "No."

The leader of the bluff people's eyes narrowed. "What do you mean, 'No'?"

"I can't let you kill him. He's not like the rest of them. I promise."

"And how do you know that?"

"What's going on?"

"Oliver!" Lennox cried out, relieved to see her brother with Easton beside him, both with weapons in hand. "It's Sky. Easton, please! Tell them it's possible to come back from this. Please, don't let them kill him."

Lennox would beg if she had to, but she shouldn't have to. Looking over her shoulder and down at Sky, she confirmed again that she saw the same eyes that she had seen in her dream. Only the outer rim of his green irises glowed. That had to mean something. He fought the Venom. He fought the darkness inside.

"Please, I am telling you Sky is still in there. I mean, look at him. He's not even moving, let alone taking control of our minds. I bet he could if he wanted to, but he's not!"

Stepping closer, both Easton and Oliver looked behind Lennox to see the fallen Sparrow on his knees.

"We can't take any chances," Easton said. "Oliver, com Ace to bring the shackles."

Chapter 15

Sky's ankles and wrists were shackled with electric chains. Blood trickled down his arm from where the arrow pierced his flesh. Unfazed by the pain, he appeared stoic with his head down and eyes toward the ground. Lennox could hardly bare to see him like this. She wanted to free him so badly, just to be with him again.

A dozen men guarded Sky, their weapons ready.

"She's unpredictable," Anthony told the men who had captured her before. "Watch her." He walked the short distance to where his men waited.

"You can't lock him up like he's some sort of animal!" Lennox pleaded.

Anthony ignored her.

Lennox shook her head, digging her nails into her palms.

Oliver and Easton cornered Anthony and spoke with him. His arms flailed as Easton's voice rose to talk over him. Oliver kept looking between Lennox, Sky, and Anthony.

Lennox waited, her nails digging farther into her palms, her eyes on Sky. His fingers fisted and released. Fisted… and released… fisted…. She remembered the gesture—an anger management technique his grandfather taught him when he was a little boy. "Look at me," she whispered. She wished he would so she could at least mouth the words "Everything is going to be okay."

He was going to be okay. *They* were going to be okay.

Ace came running. "Guys!" He spoke to Anthony's men. "They need you over there." He pointed to where some women and children hid.

The men grimaced.

"Don't worry, I'll watch her." He nodded reassuringly to them.

"Don't let her anywhere near the Prowler."

"Got it." Ace crossed his arms and took a broad stance in front of Lennox. The guards were satisfied and left her in her friend's care.

When the men were engaged in helping the women and children, she hissed, "Ace! We can't let them kill him. You know Sky is still in there somewhere! That's why he didn't try to attack me or any of us when he so easily could have." She marched forward. Ace tried to stop her, but she gave him a fierce look. She would not let anyone stand in her way. Ace had carried her away from Sky once. She would not let him do it again. "I'm going."

"How are you going to get to him?" Ace questioned. "There are over a dozen men with eyes on him right now." He picked up his step to match Lennox's hastened stride. "Just stay close, Lennox. We don't know if he is... if he's...."

"Dangerous?" Lennox looked over her shoulder, but kept walking fast.

"Well, yeah." Ace grabbed Lennox's arm. "Look. The only reason I carried you away from him before was to protect you. You know that!"

Without Ace, she would be buried under a

Regime building and lost to the war. "Ace, I...." She had no clue what to say to him.

He rolled his eyes. "Just be careful. I won't stop you again. But if he—" He cleared his throat. "I'll be close by."

Lennox nodded and spun back toward Sky, only to see Anthony yanking him away.

"Anthony!" Lennox sped up and stood face-to-face with him.

Anthony scowled. "Look, we have rules here. Rules that have kept most of us alive. You have to respect that." He let out a heavy sigh. "Easton and Oliver have already spoken with me. I get it. I really do. But we just can't trust a Prowler. That's not how it works up here." Anthony marched the silent Sky toward the same holding cell where they kept the Regime scout.

"I'm not asking you to trust him. I'm asking you to trust me."

Anthony stopped, halting Sky along with him. "Listen, you're lucky we haven't killed him already. Easton informed me he may have vital information so we're going to do what we have to do."

"What does that mean?"

"It means he's a threat and we're going to treat him like one." He jerked Sky harder.

Lennox remained beside him. "He's not a threat, Anthony. He could break out of the chains at any second if he wanted to. He could get in our minds if he wanted to. But he is not doing any of those things because he is stronger than the Venom." Lennox looked to her superiors, who stood a few yards away. "Oliver? Easton? You both know he's redeemable. Tell Anthony it's possible! God can cure even a Prowler!"

They approached.

Oliver took Lennox by the arm and pulled her to the side. He spoke softly. "Len, take a breath. We're going to figure it out, okay? You have to give these people some time. Easton and I are on your side and we're doing the best we can. We *will* figure it out. Together. And we won't let them hurt Sky in the meantime."

Lennox exhaled slowly and nodded. She jogged to catch up to Sky, who still refused to speak, even to her... but neither did he struggle against his captor, she noticed.

"Look, I don't like this idea any more than you do, but we have to do what we have to do," Anthony said.

"And what is it again that you have to do?"

"Interrogate him, just like we would any other Prowler."

Lennox knew interrogation really meant torture. "You can't be serious. He's not combative! You don't have to 'interrogate' him. I am sure I can get him to speak with me." Lennox was certain Sky was here to help them, not hurt them. "He will tell you everything you want to know."

"Lennox, I know you think that you still know who this man is, but you don't. He is not who he once was." Anthony continued forward.

"How do you know that? You know nothing about him!"

"I know he's full of Prowler Venom and that's enough, that's all I need to know about him. I am not willing to risk my people." Anthony turned to her. "Are you?" Hate filled his eyes.

Lennox stood, her mouth agape. She'd heard stories around camp about how one lone Prowler took

Anthony's wife and children. She did not blame him for his distrust of Sky. She empathized with his loss and felt his burden for his people, but this wasn't just any Prowler. This was *Sky*! There had to be something she could do that would work for all of them.

Sky finally raised his head high enough to let Lennox see his face. He shook his head, the movement so subtle she wasn't really sure it had happened.

Anthony pulled the passive Prowler into the interrogation tent.

Lennox followed.

"No." Anthony pointed to the opening of the tent, directing her away. "You can't be in here. I can't have you interfering."

"I won't. In fact, I can help keep him calm," she insisted. She would not leave Sky behind. Not again.

"Your presence won't be necessary. I have ways to keep him calm."

His words sent a chill up her spine. *Ways? What ways?* Her thoughts wandered to the darkest possibilities.

Anthony squared his shoulders. His expression—while clearly devoid of anger or

158

judgment—was set with determination. "You're too emotionally attached and your presence will only hinder our progress."

"I know his triggers," she spoke softly, changing tactics. "I can read him. I know his tells." Lennox shifted her weight, adding, "I know when he's lying."

He sighed. "You're not gonna give up, are you?"

"No."

Anthony stared her down. "Fine. But if you interfere in any sort of way, you're out of here."

"I understand."

"Good." Anthony shoved Sky onto a metal stool as Easton and Oliver entered. "Y'all ready to begin?"

Lennox's gaze flashed to Easton and her brother. Was she the only one who remembered who Sky was?

Easton moved closer. "We want answers, too."

"And there are humane ways to do that," Oliver added, his hands on his hips. "No one has to get hurt here."

Lennox let out a breath of thanks. Even in the ugliness of war, Oliver stood up for what was right and good.

"Fine. We'll try it your way first, but if he doesn't talk…."

"Understood." Oliver nodded. He took five steps more and stood directly in front of Sky.

Sky looked up, ready for Oliver's sure-to-come first question.

"Your tracker. Where is it?"

"I don't have one," Sky answered softly.

His voice quickened Lennox's heartbeat. Though his appearance changed—broader shoulders, stronger arms, yellow skin, and glowing eyes—his voice remained the same.

Easton stepped closer with a disapproving glare.

Oliver knelt down, staring at him face-to-face. "Sky, we know they track you. They track all Prowlers. With each second that passes with that thing in you, you are putting us in danger. For your own sake, please don't lie to me again."

As massive and dangerous as he was, he appeared completely vulnerable now. All his guards

160

seemed down, causing Lennox to see only the old Sky, not the Prowler that the Venom made him become.

"I'm telling the truth." Sky lifted his shackled hands and pulled at the neck of his Regime uniform. "Look." He crawled his fingers to the nape of his neck. "Here."

Lennox walked around Oliver and Easton to see his neck for herself, but stayed back, far enough to appease Anthony. A partially-healed gash about a half-inch deep resided where a tracker had been.

"I took it out as soon as I remembered it was there. No one knows I'm here. I just... I just had to make sure Lennox was okay." He glanced at Lennox. "I wanted to protect you." His gaze moved back to Oliver. "I'm so sorry. I think the mountain lion attack was my fault. They were tracking me." He looked at Anthony. "I didn't know it until it was too late, when they had already picked up my scent." His gaze swung back to Lennox. "All I wanted was to keep you safe." He lowered his head. "I'm sorry."

Lennox refused to keep her distance any longer. Ignoring Anthony's glare, she strode to his side. She knelt by Oliver and rested her hand over Sky's

161

shackled wrists.

He turned his hand over and gently grasped her fingers, giving a quick squeeze. "The Regime is coming." He took a deep breath. "I've been following them. When I saw your convoy, I knew they did, too. They've been on the move, obliterating every safe site they can. It's only a matter of time." He released her hand, tucking his into hard fists with his fingers curling around his thumbs beneath. "It's only a matter of time before they break through here, too. They've found out a way to penetrate the Sparrow technology."

"How?" Easton stepped forward.

"I don't know." Sky gazed up at her.

"What about Sparrow City?"

"Safe. For now. They've only broken through the smaller domes. From what I know, anyway." He shifted his weight. "There's one more thing."

"What?" Easton waited.

"Ahab is with them. It's some sort of publicity stunt. He broadcasts every victory, every mass grave, every evil act possible to spread fear within the defiant cities." Sky cleared his throat. "And when he finds out 'the girl who stood' is here, he will put her to death as a victory claim on this war. He won't stop until he knows for sure he's killed her." Sky turned his attention solely to Lennox. "When he finds out you're here, he's going to come for you himself."

Lennox stood up straight and squared her shoulders, courage finding residence. "Let him come." The Lord had already confirmed the word in her spirit—conquer. They would all conquer. Her pulse thumped hard inside her veins.

Sky's brows furrowed. "He won't fight fair."

"Neither will I," Lennox said without hesitation.

Anthony slammed his palms against a metal table, stopping the conversation. With all eyes on him, he shook his head forcefully. "Are you kidding me? Are y'all hearing this? So now, *now* the Regime is on their way here? Ahab, the devil himself, is coming with a vendetta against you?" He pointed to Lennox and narrowed his eyes. "What then? We prepare for war on the bluffs? We are sitting ducks up here!"

"How much longer do you think we have?" Oliver breathed deeply.

"One, maybe two days. A Regime brigade has

been on the move for the past week. Once word gets to them about this campsite and Lennox's presence, it won't take them long. You have their scout. You have me. They'll come for us. They'll come for Lennox." Sky unfurled his fingers one-by-one and then clenched them again into tight balls. "But what they don't know is that you have a weapon."

"What weapon? We don't have a weapon to stop an army!" Anthony shouted.

"You have me." Sky glanced at each of the four faces in front of him, stopping at Lennox's. "I can do things others can't."

"You mean, they don't know you've turned?" Easton spoke from behind Sky.

Sky looked over his shoulder. "No, no one knows. The mountain lions were following my trail. That's what they're trained to do. They follow Prowlers."

"And how do we know this isn't a trap?" Anthony folded his arms. "Maybe you're playing us, setting us up."

"Because if I wanted to hurt you, I would have already." He broke the chains that bound his wrists by pulling his fists apart. They fell to the ground with a light thud. "Believe me now?"

Anthony stood slack-jawed and he uncrossed his arms. "Okay, but that doesn't mean I trust you."

"I don't blame you." Sky lowered his head once again and placed his hands on his lap, palms up. "Tie me up again if it makes you feel better."

Lennox reached for Sky's hand while looking at Anthony. "He won't hurt your people. He's not like the rest of them."

"All I've got is an eighteen-year-old girl's word to vouch for a Prowler with Venom in his veins?" Anthony furrowed his brows. "A Prowler just like him took my two children and my wife. I don't know if I can do this. I just don't know."

"He will help to protect us. I'm sure of it. And I know it's only my word, but you have it."

"And mine." Oliver stood tall.

"Mine, as well," Easton said, crossing her arms. "Anthony, Sky is the secret weapon we've always wished we had against the Regime. I believe God sent him to us and now he will help us get through this."

"Well, God help us all then." Anthony shook

his head and turned to leave. "God help us all."

Chapter 16

In the interrogation tent, Lennox kept a tight hold on Sky's hand as Oliver paced and Easton feverishly wrote down coordinates to nearby safe sites.

"We will never make it to another Sparrow safe site." Easton tapped the end of the pencil on the table. "Not with all these people. It's too far. We need to come up with home advantage."

"At least we know they're coming," Oliver offered.

"I'm afraid that won't be enough." Easton set a hologram projector on a stack of crates. After tapping a few buttons, a three-dimensional grid of the bluffs appeared. "There aren't many, but there are ways the Regime has found to penetrate our defenses." She pointed to several areas on the grid.

Oliver turned to Sky. "Do you know how they'll approach?"

"When Ahab feels threatened, he attacks on all fronts—both from the air and on the ground. We'll see the air strikes coming, but there won't be much we can do about them, unless you have the weapons to bring them down."

"I don't, but I know who does." Easton typed on her tech screen. "I'm sending an encrypted message to Sia and Max. They can get us what we need."

"In time?" Lennox asked.

"I sure hope so. What's the plan on the ground, Sky? How many can you hold off at a time?"

"Prowlers take more effort, of course. I've never fought more than five at a time and that was in a controlled lab experiment, but I can focus on them while you hold off the soldiers."

"What about your shoulder?" Lennox narrowed her gaze.

"Already healing." Sky pulled the neck of his uniform to the side so she could see.

"We'll need supplies." Oliver studied the grid and tapped his index finger on the crates.

"I'll go," Lennox said.

"Take Sky with you an—"

Anthony barged into the tent. A multitude of shouting men and arguing women stood just outside. Beads of sweat poured from his hairline and his face contorted into an uncomfortable looking frown, as if he was distraught or tempted beyond his threshold. "Listen, I talked to my people. They will never accept him. They will never accept his help." He held a revolver in his right hand.

Easton rested her hand on her weapon with a calm disposition, ready to draw. "All due respect, sir, it's the only way we stand a chance."

Anthony shook his head violently. "As much as I hate to admit it, I know that, but he can't be here. My people don't and won't understand." His left hand trembled at his side. "My family wasn't the only one taken that night the Prowler broke through our defenses." He raised his gun. "I'm sorry. I have to... I have to kill him. It's the only way now."

"What? No!" Lennox slid her body in front of Sky, but he moved her out of the way just as fast.

A simple sweep of his hand thwarted her efforts

to protect him. "Lennox, it's okay." He stood in front of her now, hands raised in surrender… again.

Easton slowly positioned herself to disarm Anthony, one step at a time.

Anthony's bloodshot eyes darted to Sky, who stood still. Anthony blinked hard twice, his hand securely on the trigger. "I'm sorry."

"Anthony, don't." Oliver stepped in front of the gun with his right hand out, throwing Anthony off guard.

"Get out of my way, Oliver."

"He is not the enemy. Not anymore."

Sky moved closer, drawing attention back to himself until the gun was rightfully placed at its intended target. "Anthony, I hate what I am more than you do. I fight it every second of every minute. I promise you, I will not hurt anyone, and I will do everything in my power to not let anyone hurt your people ever again."

"I just don't know what else to do. You can't be here." Anthony's voice rose in pitch, shaking almost as much as the gun in his hand.

"Take it easy," Oliver said, approaching

Anthony with his hands up. "It doesn't have to be this way. We can think of something else."

"My men want him dead. Now." He refused to comply and shook his head frantically. "I don't have a choice."

"Everyone has a choice." Oliver took one step closer. "We need him. He's an asset, not an enemy." He cautiously took another step, then another, hands still up.

"Yeah, I tried to explain that to them. It did not go over well." Anthony sidestepped to see past Oliver and re-aimed his shaking gun at Sky.

"I'll leave." Sky took a step back. "And I won't come back. I'm sorry for the trouble I've caused."

Understanding dawned on Anthony's face. "But *they're* really coming, aren't they?" He rubbed his forehead and wiped the sweat from his face. "And we can't do it without you, can we?" Anthony came to his senses. He finally lowered the gun and let out an exasperated sigh.

Sky cautiously dropped his hands. "They are coming and I don't know if we all can hold them off. I just know you have a better chance with me."

Anthony's forehead creased as he raised his eyes to Sky. "My men won't accept your help."

Sky's expression sobered. "They don't have to know. I will fight the Regime from down below. Stop them from ever coming up the bluff. Your people won't ever see me. I'm good at disappearing."

Lennox raised a questioning brow. "How? How can you do that by yourself, Sky? You're strong, but not invincible. You said yourself you can only hold off five Prowlers." He would be a bigger target than she was once the Regime realized he fought against them.

"We can hold them off together," Sky replied. "Sparrows can cover the edges at the top of the bluff. I will patrol the bottom."

"*We'll* patrol the bottom with you," Oliver confirmed. "You can't do that alone, not even as a Prowler."

"We fight together, or we flee together," Lennox agreed.

"I can't let y'all do that." Even more concern took over Sky's already hard-pressed features.

"Since when did we need your permission?" Lennox arched an eyebrow as if to say, "You can't stop

172

me even if you tried."

The four Sparrows looked to Anthony.

"Will this work?" Easton asked.

Anthony nodded his head and rubbed his chin. "Only if they think he's dead." He raised his gun once again and took aim.

BANG!

The noise of the blast echoed throughout the campsite. The bullet hit a sack of rice next to him. White grains spilled out from the hole as the crowd outside roared a cheer of victory

"Go," Anthony commanded.

Easton nodded. "I'll prepare the teams up here and they'll get his men ready."

"You two gather supplies. We'll meet you guys by the pond." Oliver thrust his chin up. "Hurry."

Lennox understood and led Sky to the back opening of the large canvas tent. Together, they slipped into the darkness that fell over camp.

"This way." She led him across a small, empty space on the bluff and to the next tent over. Too many people still wandered around the opening of the other tent to the left. "What do you think they're waiting for?"

"Proof?" Sky peered back to the people who so badly wanted him dead. "I sure hope Anthony can explain why my corpse isn't lying on the ground."

"I'm sure they'll think of something. They're very resourceful," Lennox reassured. She moved swiftly forward with Sky right behind her. "We need to get to that tent over there." She pointed to one with a red sparrow painted on the top. "It's got all of the supplies we'll need."

Sky mouthed the words "Follow me," and before Lennox could say anything else, he bolted to the tent. His body was a mere blur to the natural eye. He waved to her, motioning for her to come.

"Nice," she said as she walked briskly to the tent. She kept her head down, not daring to make eye contact if anyone should pass by her, and ran the last five feet. "I forgot you could move like that," Lennox said, hiding behind the supply tent with him.

He smiled. "It's about the only thing the Venom did that I am actually thankful for." He scanned the perimeter and listened intently. "It's clear. I don't detect anyone inside." He slid the opening and held it open for Lennox to glide through.

Discretely, Lennox and Sky rummaged around the supply tent. Lennox turned her headlamp on to see and packed up the extra ammunition, medical supplies, and any Sparrow tech she found. She opened a wooden crate and fumbled her hand over its contents.

Breaking the silence, Sky whispered, "Lennox?"

She stopped searching. "Yeah?"

"I have to tell you something." He waited.

"What? Is everything okay?" She lifted her head, shining the light in his direction, which made his eyes glimmer.

"You know that dream you had?"

Her heart pounded. She had many dreams. She scrunched her nose, letting out a small huff, thankful for the darkness hiding the heat that rushed her cheeks. *Which one?* she thought, for she had too many to count—ones that consisted of her finding him again and again.

The glowing rim around Sky's irises brightened. "The one where I dragged you out of the tent and spoke to you as we sat on that rock."

"What!? How do you even kn—"

"It was real."

Of course, that was how a piece of her mother's locket got there!

He continued. "You know the Venom gives Prowlers these crazy abilities to control the mind, right? Well, I learned how to get in your head while you were sleeping without taking full control."

"You mean…."

"Everything we talked about was real. All of it." He paused a brief moment. "Lennox, while I was on their operating table, as they poked and prodded me and filled my veins with Venom, two things screamed within my soul. One…" he took a step toward her, "I knew I had to find my way back to God, first and foremost, and two…" another step closer, "I had to find my way back to you."

Lennox turned into his waiting arms. "I've missed you so much!" She brought the scuffed piece of gold jewelry out. "I got the message. I did not know what to believe. I thought I was going crazy!"

"You weren't going crazy. I was there and I thought you might want the locket back, even just a small piece of it. To remember …"

She closed her fingers around the gold. "You were right."

Sky pressed his lips to hers with a sweet, tender kiss. When he pulled away, he rested his forehead against hers and said, "I just had to make sure you were okay." He pulled her closer. "But I also had to know if you *did* see me again, that you… that you would accept me." He shook his head. "It wasn't fair to do that to you. I'm sorry. I love you, Lennox."

A tear ran down her cheek. "I love you too." She rested her forehead against the bridge of his nose. "I always have. Always will."

He inhaled deeply and exhaled slowly. "I had no idea how telling you would make me feel…."

"And how does it make you feel?"

He released her and moved his hands to her cheeks, gently sweeping his thumbs across her cheekbones. "Free."

Lennox's heart leapt. She remembered what he'd said in her dream, but now he was free. He found his way back to God through the darkness and God allowed him to find her. *Thank You, God!*

A commotion outside the tent stole the moment.

"*Shh!*" Sky lifted a finger to his mouth.

If anyone saw Sky, their plan was ruined. The camp had to believe Sky was dead.

Voices belonging to young men filled the air. Sky stood motionless. Lennox turned off her headlamp and waited.

The canvas flap at the entrance opened and a silhouette of a man came in to view. He snuck in like he tried to hide, too. Sky grabbed Lennox's arm and pulled her to a crouching position beside him.

"Lennox?" the silhouette whispered. "Are you in here?"

Lennox turned to Sky. "It's Ace." She started to stand but Sky's voice pulled her attention back down.

"Can we trust him?" he asked, standing slowly.

"Yes," Lennox reassured. She trusted him with her life. "Ace, what are you doing here?"

Ace walked closer. "I'm seeing if y'all need any help. I heard what's about to happen." He shined a small light at the two of them and his eyes lingered on Sky. "Sky, I... um—"

"No worries." Sky stepped around the table and

offered his hand. "You did what you had to do."

Ace clasped his hand around Sky's and drew him in. "You're my brother."

"And you're mine," Sky agreed.

Lennox hated breaking up the moment. "Guys, we better get back to it. We don't have much time."

Sky nodded in agreement.

"What can I do?" Ace asked.

Lennox contemplated taking him with them, but ultimately decided against it. "Easton is giving the orders for all Sparrows to stay topside. We need a guy like you up here, Ace. She knows we will need snipers, especially with your skills above us." Going against orders never panned out. "You'll serve all of us best up top."

Ace nodded in agreement and held out his arms. "In case we don't see each other again."

Lennox met his embrace and returned his bear hug. "We'll see each other when it's all over. I know we will." She pressed her cheek against his chest and let his uniform absorb her tears.

Ace held out his right arm. "Get in here again, man. Group hug!"

Sky chuckled and wrapped his arms around them both.

After a moment, Lennox lifted her voice, "Heavenly Father," she prayed over them, "guide and protect us as we fight. May Your will be done on Earth as it is in Heaven. In Jesus' name, amen."

"Amen," Sky and Ace echoed. After one final big squeeze, they parted.

"Let's take down the devil and his goons, shall we?" Ace grinned. "I'll keep watch and make sure to steer the campsite's attention away from you guys. Shouldn't be too hard."

"Thank you," Lennox said. "Be safe."

A pearly-white smile spread across his face. "You don't have to fear the dark when you walk in the light, right?" With that, he patted Sky's shoulder and walked out of the tent.

"He's a good guy," Sky said as he dove back into preparations.

"Yeah, he is." Lennox turned her headlamp back on and gathered the necessary equipment too, making sure to leave enough for the Sparrows who were to stay atop.

"I'm glad he was there for you when I…." He trailed off and sighed. "I thought maybe you and Ace had, you know, um—"

"He's a good friend," Lennox stated. "Nothing more. I never stopped caring for you, hoping for your return. Not once."

He smiled, placing a light hand on her cheek. "I never stopped thinking about you, either." He gently leaned in, pressing his lips to hers. "I never want to have to be without you again."

"Me neither." Lennox threw her arms around his neck and hugged him tight, wanting to never let him go, but the commotion outside told her she had to for now. "Ready?"

"Ready." Sky heaved his bulky pack as if it weighed nothing, its weight would surely be impossible for any other man to carry. "Let's finish this."

Lennox turned on her night vision. "Let's go." She led the way, walking first, then jogging. Her supply pack hit against her tailbone with each step. She wasn't too worried they would be followed, but when she turned to make sure Sky was still behind her, she noticed he, too, glanced backward.

"Good?" she asked. Her night vision goggles picked up the glow of his eyes and in even his skin.

"Good," he nodded.

Lennox decided to pass on the other side of the bluff to avoid the foxhole where there were sure to be the camp's soldiers. She could explain it to Frankie and Martin, anyone else, she wasn't so sure.

"Just a little bit farther." Lennox picked up the pace. By the pond, a man's silhouette caused her to pause. She slowed, cautiously.

Sky took the lead "It's Oliver."

Right. His enhanced senses were better than hers, even with the night vision goggles.

Oliver stood on the outer bank. "You guys got everything?"

"Yeah. All we could carry, anyway." Lennox gestured to her pack. "Where's Easton?"

"She'll be here soon." Oliver set his pack on the ground, sitting down beside it. "Until then, we wait."

Thirty minutes passed before a slim figure approached the pond at a run.

"It's Easton," Sky confirmed.

"Reinforcements are coming," Easton said

182

when she caught her breath. "They're positioning a satellite to defend the bluff from being completely annihilated."

"How long before Sparrow reinforcements arrive on the ground?" Oliver stood again, picked up his pack and adjusted the straps.

"Two days, but once the satellite is positioned the shield will help stave damage from airstrikes until they arrive."

"Can we hold them off that long?" Oliver questioned.

Easton let out a deep breath. "We have to."

"You remember what dad said?" Lennox looked at Oliver. "'It's in the face of opposition that you'll find what you are truly made of.'" Lennox slid her thumbs beneath the straps of her pack and wrapped her others around them, fortified by remembering her father's words. "Let's find out what we are made of, shall we?"

Chapter 17

With Sky's surefootedness to guide their foot placement along the narrow, unsure path, the trek down the bluff was much easier than coming up had been.

When they reached the bottom, Easton wasted no time, immediately listing off orders. "Oliver and I will cover the south and west ends of the bluffs, leaving you and Sky to cover the north and east. Got it?"

"Got it," Lennox confirmed.

"Sky?"

"Got it." He gave a thumb's up.

"From here forward, we are radio silent. We can't chance the Regime intercepting our transmissions." Oliver acted sure of the plan, but his tone suggested otherwise.

"Understood." Lennox turned off her com. They

had to keep the element of surprise. With a nod to her and then to Sky, Oliver and Easton disappeared behind a curve of rock.

"They're going to be fine," Sky soothed, as if he read her thoughts.

Could he? She faced him. "Can you read my thoughts?"

"I wish." Sky laughed a little. "Or... maybe I don't. Either way, I'm not that good, yet. Just dreams and fear-control stuff so far." He searched the trees around them. "You should get some sleep, Easton's orders. We need to be well rested before they come. I'm sure it will be a long fight." He led her to a nook in a dead, hollow tree. "Climb inside. I'll keep watch."

"What about you?"

"I don't need much rest." He lifted a hand to the back of his neck.

"Are you sure?"

He cupped her cheeks in his strong hands. "I'm sure."

Lennox tilted her head, leaning into his hand as she gazed into his caring eyes.

Oh, how she loved him.

"Go. Rest." He gentled the command with a kiss to the tip of her nose.

She answered with a kiss to his chin and then crawled inside the hollow tree. Inside, she was able to sit upright, cocooned in safety. Rest did not come easily. She wrestled with her thoughts, shifting back and forth for what felt like hours before finally drifting off.

A drop of sweat tickled as it traced a path down her temple, waking her to a soft hazy glow that whispered the arrival of a new day. Sticking her head out of the hollow tree, she checked her surroundings and then cautiously wriggled the rest of her body out. Standing, she stretched her limbs and then adjusted her gear, reactivating the Kev disk on her sleeve that she must have bumped off in the middle of the night. She scanned along the bottom of the bluffs for Sky, alert to any unusual sounds or movement.

There he was, not too far from her.

It was eerie the valley. The trees and shrubbery stood at attention and the surrounding bluffs towered over them, casting giant shadows.

Sky jogged toward her.

"Any movement?" she asked, looking off into the distance. Only the wind swayed the dead branches and stirred the earth.

"Not yet." Sky secured the strap to his Stryker and threw it over his shoulder.

She met his gaze and her breath stuttered over the beauty of his eyes, the glow even more stunning in the daylight. She pushed the thought away. She couldn't be distracted from their purpose.

The ghostly wild was not welcoming. *How much longer?* her mind wondered. "They're close though, aren't they?"

Sky's jaw tensed for a brief second. "We'll be ready for them," he nodded.

Together, they patrolled the outer rim of the north side of the bluffs, surveying the land with weapons at the ready.

The sun positioned itself right above them, declaring it almost noon. There was still no sign of the Regime, but just as Lennox had believed in her soul that Sky was alive, she felt the darkness thicken around them. It was as if evil was an actual beast and it roamed the air, searching the hearts of men. Ahab was close. She knew it. This was the calm before the storm.

Sky pointed to a mound of shrubbery in the distance. Lennox followed him to it. Crouching down, Sky tested his vantage point by aiming his gun and checking his scope. He twisted his neck as if it were sore. When he met her gaze, his calm visage settled into something both determined and concerned. "The first wave is here."

Lennox crouched beside him and looked around for evidence. "How do you know?"

"I can hear them."

"How many?"

"Maybe a dozen. I can't tell, exactly. They're in heavy utility vehicles… two miles out." He listened more intently. "They'll be coming from the east. They'll be in sight in less than three minutes."

Lennox's heart pounded. *Lord, help us.* She readied her Stryker and waited.

The minutes dragged, ticking away until they finally revealed the Regime caravan. Two trucks with canvas-covered backs drove right past the shrubs

Lennox and Sky hid behind. The drivers skidded the vehicles to a stop at the base of the bluff, where their cargo of men piled out with tactical gear on and weapons drawn.

As the enemy eyed the land around them, Lennox counted. "You were right. There's twelve of them."

"No Prowlers." Sky peered through his scope. "Take down the ones on your left. I'll take the right. On three. One…."

Lennox steadied her weapon and held it in line with her target.

"Two…."

Inhale.

"Three."

Exhale.

Sky and Lennox fired simultaneous rounds. One-by-one, Regime soldiers fell, twisting in agony as blue serum coursed through their veins. Two men in black bolted behind the vehicles, shooting aimlessly into the distance. As their bullets whizzed past the shrubs, Lennox made herself smaller by tucking her head and shoulders down. Sky remained up, keeping his gun pointed.

"There are still two left." Lennox fired another round.

"I see them. We aren't going to be able to get them at this angle while they're behind the truck. I'll take control of their minds and coax them out, you take the shot?" Sky looked to Lennox and raised his brows.

She nodded and set her sights again, aiming her weapon by the front end of the Humvee. She glanced at Sky.

He closed his eyes, took a deep breath, and reopened them. The glowing rim around his irises expanded. He grit his teeth and tightened his jaw. "Now."

Both men wandered out from behind the protection of the truck, swatting at imaginary fears in front of them. Lennox remembered all too well the control a Prowler had over its victim.

She fired the first shot, bringing the largest of the men down first, and then pointed her barrel at the other, firing the second shot. Down he went, veins glowing blue. She did a quick count. A small army of men lay crumpled on the dirt. "Is that all of them?"

Sky stood up and scanned the area. "Yes. But it won't be long until the others arrive. They know we're here." The muscles of his jawline ticked. "And... I can sense Ahab."

A chill ran down her spine. It had been a long time since she had seen the man responsible for this war, a man so consumed by the devil that he'd lost all sense of humanity, decency, and compassion. Her muscles tensed and her heart thumped against her ribs. If Ahab was close, the time for judgment had come.

She glanced at Sky. It seemed almost poetic that the very weapon Ahab created would be the one that would destroy him.

Chapter 18

Blades chopped the air above and Lennox and Sky dove for cover.

When it came closer, Lennox barely made out the emblem of a red sparrow painted on the tail of the helicopter. "The reinforcements are here!"

"They're early. I—" Sky paused. "Lennox, get down!"

Before she could react to the command, Sky tackled her to the ground, covering her body with his own. In her peripheral vision, Lennox watched as the helicopter exploded into a dozen pieces, forming a dark cloud of thick smoke overhead. Flaming metal fell all around them. Lennox gasped as the rest of the helicopter spun like a tornado to the earth. Bullets hit the ground, sending chunks of dirt and rock flying as two Regime jets whistled by overhead.

"We have to move." Sky pulled Lennox up and jolted her forward.

Screaming pain shot up from her heel to her knee as she put pressure on her left leg. Her fall must have deactivated her Kev disk at the wrong time. She bit her bottom lip and pushed through the pain, pressing the disk to make sure it reactivated.

"I can hear reinforcements coming, but I can also hear more Regime vehicles approaching too. More of them than I anticipated." He tucked her closer to the base of the bluffs. "We can't let their foot soldiers up there."

Lennox wracked her brain. "Could we use their trucks to block the path?"

"Tell me what you're thinking."

"We can drive their trucks into the rock and set them on fire. It's only a temporary hold, but worth a shot." If it played out like it had in her brain, it would work for a short time. "You think the bluff is stable enough?"

"Yeah, I do, let's do it." Sky ran to a Regime truck and started the engine.

Lennox sprinted to the other, trying to hide the pain as she moved. Sky positioned his first, driving one wheel right on the ramp, and hopped out. The utility truck teetered diagonally. Lennox rammed hers into the side of it to secure the first one's place. She hobbled out and pulled two hand grenades from her pack, handing one to Sky. Both pulled the clips and threw the explosives into their designated vehicles and ran back, anticipating the blast. The two enemy vehicles burst into flames after the initial explosion.

"That should hold them off for a little bit." Sky watched the fire. The orange and yellow wisps reflected off his eyes. Shouts were heard in the distance.

"Come on!" Sky sprinted to the hollowed out tree, but Lennox limped behind him, gritting her teeth to keep from crying out when the muscles in her left leg refused to cooperate.

Sky glanced back and was at her side in a flash, helping her to safety within a copse of shrubs. "You're hurt! What happened?"

"Nothing. I'm fine."

His scowl said he didn't believe her, but a

194

second later, Sky tilted his head to the side. "Ahab's close." He wrinkled his nose and the glow of his irises thickened. "I can smell his awful cologne." Sky looked off into the distance then to Lennox. "Stay here and don't give up your location. I'll call when the time is right." He cradled her face in his hands. "I love you."

He sprinted behind a hunk of blazing metal.

Lennox readied her Stryker and forced oxygen to cycle through her lungs. In, and out.

Another Regime caravan rolled near. As the utility vehicles stopped, a group of soldiers hopped out, just like before. This time, however, there were five groups instead of two. Three Prowlers jumped to the ground from the last Humvee. Their eyes were wild— more beast than man. Lennox thanked God Sky had not turned out like them.

One Prowler stuck his nose in the air and sniffed like a dog. The others followed suit. It pointed to the others and they headed straight for Sky.

Sky, get out of there! Lennox bit the inside of her cheek, tempted to shoot at them, but that would definitely give up her location. *Come on, Sky.*

The three crept closer to his position. Five more

seconds and they'd be right on top of him. One… two… three… four…. The Prowlers grabbed their heads and fell to their knees.

Sky did it! He was in their heads. He stepped out from behind the debris and fired three rounds, one Sparrow bullet for each Prowler. They lit up bright blue as the serum entered their veins.

The men at the Humvees turned and raised their weapons at Sky.

"Now!" Sky yelled.

Lennox aimed her weapon at the active soldiers. Four went down. She rose, limping closer as Sky advanced.

Out of nowhere, a group of arrows whistled through the air. Several Regime soldiers fell as the wooden arrows found their marks.

Lennox glanced back and estimated the starting point of the arrows' trajectory. She saw Elise—along with a few boys—ducking behind a chunk of blown-up helicopter. Ignoring the pain in her leg, she offered cover fire and made her way to the redhead and her team of archers. "What are you guys doing out here? Y'all are going to get yourselves killed!"

Elise loosed an arrow. It arched high before screaming down into a Regime soldier's shoulder. "We heard about the plan and wanted to help."

"It's too dangerous for you down here," Lennox admonished while scanning for threats. A few men tried to tether a pulley to move the transports out of the way. Lennox readied her weapon and fired. Three shots brought down three soldiers. Lennox hunkered down and looked to Elise again, who pulled an arrow from her quiver. "How'd you get down here, anyway?"

"Where there's a will, there's a way." She nocked an arrow. "We rappelled down," she shrugged. "We've done it dozens of times."

"Can you get back up?" Lennox leaned out and fired off another round, but was forced to tuck back in and take cover from the bullets that flew back. "Y'all should go back up where it's safe."

Elise glanced over her shoulder. "C'mon, Lennox. Nowhere is safe." She looked to Lennox. "I'd rather do something brave and die than hide and die. I want to fight. *Please*, let us fight." She strengthened her posture. "God is with us, we shall not fail. His Word never fails."

She remembered what it was like to be in Elise's shoes. "I can't argue with that." Who was she to stop these kids from fighting for what they believed? "You're archers, so you can stay back. Fight from a distance. Sky and I will take the lead."

"Got it," Elise nodded.

Lennox peeked toward the battle. Sky took out the majority of the enemies by himself, it seemed. But there were so many. And likely more on the way.

"One more thing." Lennox took the Sparrow disk off her suit and put it on Elise. The protective nanotubes formed around Elise's body, from her feet all the way up to her fiery red hair. Her light green eyes widened. "I ca—"

"You can, and you will. If I had more, I'd give each of you one, but with the shortage…." Lennox remembered the new invention she placed in her pocket from Sia and Max. Her hands searched her suit and pulled out the small silver bullet-shaped tech. "Here." She held out the new tech to Elise. "It's a personal dome. Extra protection for your guys. All they have to do is press it and it will shield them. It doesn't last long, but it's better than nothing."

Elise wrapped her fingers around it. "Thank you."

Lennox nodded and then leaned several inches forward to check her position. If she ran fast, it would take less than a minute to get to where Sky fought several men. She just had to make sure she did not get shot first.

A rainstorm of heavy artillery emerged as the Regime pressed harder against their defense. Pings of bullets hitting shredded metal filled Lennox's ears. She inhaled deeply and pushed herself out from behind the safety of the metal. She heard the bullets whiz by her head as they found residence in the dirt and debris around her. She ducked behind a rotten and twisted tree that had breathed its last breath a long time ago. Sneaking a glance at the enemy before her, she made a fast break to another large piece of debris right next to Sky. He seized their minds and she took them down with Sparrow serum.

Lennox took out the last Regime soldier they could see. "Is that all of them?"

"For now." Sky crouched down behind his makeshift barricade.

The blasts and gunfire ceased, leaving the sound of crackling fire and groaning men as the only noises. The stillness did not sit well with Lennox's soul. She dug her nails into her palms, forming tiny half-moons in her skin. "It's too quiet out there."

The glowing ring around Sky's irises thinned. "The calm before the *real* fight begins." He clenched his jaw. "Something bigger is coming. I can feel it in every single bone." Letting out a heavy breath, he stood and listened, his eyes glazing over as he did. He jutted his chin to the south, mouthing the words, "Over there."

A pillar of smoke rose high in the air from the territory Oliver and Easton were covering. Lennox pulled out her binoculars. A group of Regime soldiers marched forward in the distance. They moved as ants, working with one another in unison. "Whoever Oliver and Easton can't take down will be coming straight for us."

The sky shifted, forming dark shades of red and orange-gray clouds.

"Look." Lennox pointed up. She stared as the angry colors swirled together. Had the earth finally had enough and decided to consume itself?

Drip.

One drop fell.

Drip. Drip.

Then another, and another.

Lennox wiped the water from her face with her left hand, looking down at it as she did.

Red rain.

Sky turned to her.

The droplets multiplied until they teemed down on them. Soon, the patter of footfalls caused both Lennox and Sky to raise their weapons and spin wildly around. Elise and her boys with bows and arrows in hand stood before them, soaking wet. Both Lennox and Sky lowered their weapons.

"What's going on?" Elise asked. The rain plastered her red hair to her face like suffocating bloody tendrils. Tech flickered. "The Regime is gone. I don't see any more of them coming."

"Not gone," Sky said, pointing into the distance. "They're out there."

"And the blood-red rain?" a boy soldier asked. He could not have been any older than twelve.

"I don't know, but I'm pretty sure it has something to do with the GWS shutting down." Lennox swallowed hard. It smelled like sulfur mixed with iron—stronger than anything she'd ever smelled in a ward before.

One of Elise's boys stared at Sky, finally blurting out, "I'm sorry I shot you." He cowered and hung his head low.

Sky smiled. "I forgive you. You were scared and you didn't know who I was. I probably would have done the same." Sky gently lifted the boy's chin. "Listen, what matters is that you guys stay safe." He turned to Lennox. "It's going to get worse. I don't know if I can protect all of them."

"You don't have to," Elise said, repositioning her quiver on her back.

Sky's eyes shifted to a smaller set of bluffs farther off. "Quiet." He held up a finger to silence even the youngest of boys. He focused on the perimeter. "I've heard that sound before." There was more than a hint of worry in his voice. He squeezed his eyes shut and the muscles in his neck visibly tensed. He sucked in a breath and his eyes popped open, "They're preparing the mortars."

Chapter 19

Within seconds of Sky's warning, a massive orange ball of fury flew through the sky. Fiery wisps illuminated a darkening backdrop, one after the other. Fire rained down, sizzling through blood-red drops of water—the grand picture of Armageddon, painted one brush stroke at a time right before Lennox's eyes.

One missile landed far off, exploding on impact and sending a wave of heat through the valley between the bluffs. It lit up the world around her like fireworks on Independence Day. More flew up and found their way down.

Lennox swallowed her natural urge to be afraid and prayed. *Lord, protect us and the people on top. Be our defense.*

A prickling sensation spread across her skin and

every hair was raised on her arms. Time paused. Nothing moved forward. Nothing moved . . . at all. Lennox heard her own breathing. Out of the corner of her eye, she saw motion.

Wings danced up and down—delicate, beautiful, and surreal. As time ceased, her heartbeats slowed. She turned and watched a small red sparrow land on a piece of metal with fire all around it. Its grace and innocence contrasted with this war-stricken place. The bird chirped once before it cocked its head to the side, looking directly at Lennox. It flew off, straight into the direction of the Regime.

Lennox threw her head back and let the rain fall on her face. She knew God was with them. He always had been.

BOOM!

The earth shook. The dirt beneath Lennox's feet rumbled in protest. Heat coursed her veins just as much as the physical heat from the flames. Sweat poured down her skin.

Breathe. She had to remind herself, for she held her breath for too long.

Blazing shrapnel flew in all directions as a blast

went off a few yards in front of her.

"Take cover!" Sky shouted. He grabbed Lennox by the wrist, pulling her closer to him behind a boulder.

She reached in her pack and pulled out the Sapphire Shield, activating it. It formed into a crystal-clear protective barrier. Elise and the boys huddled close together and launched the personal dome Lennox had given them. The invisible tech flickered for a moment before sealing itself over the group.

"We don't have much time. I can sense over half a dozen advanced Prowlers just a few miles out. It won't be long until…" Sky shook his head. He allowed it to fall with his eyes cast down.

"Until what?" Lennox placed a hand over his wrist, grabbing hold of his attention. "Until what, Sky?"

"There are too many of them for me to hold off. I-I'm sorry. It's impossible." His gaze looked hopeless, as if he believed they were going to die here.

We're not going out like this. We can't. We won't. Had God not provided a sign of hope, only moments ago? She would stand on that truth, even if there was nothing else to stand on. "How much longer until they reach us?"

Sky furrowed his brow. "Five more minutes, give or take."

Lennox had never seen such desperation in his face. Even with all of his man-made power, his Venom abilities could not save them, and he knew it.

"We won't be overcome." Lennox squeezed her hand around his wrist, wanting to reassure Sky as God had just reassured her. Even in the simplicity of nature, God spoke. The sparrow was a sign, especially now. *Nothing is impossible.* "To live is gain and to die is gain."

Lennox released his hand slowly and stood. She had to go. Now.

Sky pulled her back down. "What are you doing?" Worry took over his face.

"We can't wait for them to get any closer. We need to stop them now, before it's too late." The words from her mother's locket—taken from God's Word— tied themselves to her course. *We walk by faith, not by sight.* Her cause was to live for more than only herself. It was to fight for more than what she could see. Lennox drew in a long breath. "You hold the Prowlers,

I'll sneak closer and take out as many men as I can."

"Lennox...." Sky's eyes dimmed almost completely back to normal. He pulled her back to him, holding her by the hand. "That won't work."

"It has to." She swallowed hard, trying to push down the lump forming in her throat. "We can hold them off at least until more Sparrows arrive. We walk by faith, not by sight. We can do this! We *have* to do this."

A mixture of adrenaline and faith pulsed through her with the strength of a river, swelling after a heavy rain. It pushed her forward, washing away doubt. The consequences she faced for being a Defier were a crown of glory on her head, and she wore it proudly. She had only pure faith now, and faith required risk—a risk she knew was worth taking.

She gazed into Sky's eyes, unwavering. "We're going to take out Ahab once and for all."

"And what exactly are you going to do again?"

"I don't know what I'll do when I get there, but I'm trusting God to reveal it and enable me to accomplish His purpose." Lennox paused and knelt beside him again. "You have to let me go." She pressed her forehead to his. "It's the only way this will work." She leaned back on her heels. Her leg miraculously felt better. The bravery and trust she had in God and His ability reinforced itself and wrapped around her like a warm blanket, providing peace. She stood taller. "I have to help my brother and Easton. They need our help. Besides, what am I here for if not to fight?"

Sky tried to smile and slowly relinquished her hand, fighting her efforts no more. "Be careful." His eyes glistened and jawline tightened. "Wait, Len, I can't get too close or the other Prowlers will…"

Lennox nodded. She understood Prowlers sensed their own stronger than anyone else. She urged him not to say another word. Chances were, they still did not know Sky fought with the Sparrows instead of against them, but as soon as he held the other Prowlers' minds, that upper-hand would be gone. They'd be exposed and Sky would be in imminent danger.

The glow increased in Sky's irises. He cocked his head to the side and pointed to his ear to indicate he was listening. "I'll hold off as many as I can when the timing is right."

"I know you will." She rose completely,

securing her pack and positioning her Stryker in front of her. "Keep Elise and the boys safe?" Lennox already knew he would because that was who he was, but she had to say it.

"Of course." Sky dipped his chin. "If they're as stubborn as you are, they'll be protecting me, too."

Lennox half-smiled.

She forced her right foot to take the first step. As she walked away from Sky, Elise, and the boys by placing one booted foot in front of the other, she moved closer to the Regime. She glimpsed back over her shoulder as she trailed farther and farther away. Sky remained steadily focused on her and her movements, while the band of young Defiers positioned themselves for combat. She faced forward again, breathed in deeply, and exhaled slowly.

Her plan had to work, just long enough for more Sparrows to arrive, even if that meant she sacrificed her own life in the process. The cause was bigger than her—bigger than the Regime—bigger than any of them.

After minutes of plowing through wreckage and blazing brush, she found herself tucked behind a forest of living trees. Limbs scratched against her wet Sparrow uniform as drops of moisture from the leaves spilled onto her face. She wiped the red rain away with a quick swipe of the back of her hand. She hid herself farther behind a tree as a Regime truck rolled passed her. It stopped over fifty feet ahead of her position.

Still hidden, she raised her binoculars and scanned left to right while counting her targets. Then, she realized they were too numerous to count. It was a vast army with only one man she knew by name.

Ahab.

He wore his usual impeccable suit with blood-red lining and square-tipped dress shoes. His sunken eyes reviewed the landscape and a wretched smile spilled across his face. She hated his crooked smile. The way it curved, darkening his eyes and jutting out his chin. Everything about him, she hated. But that smile... it was so self-assured, as if he didn't have a single care in the world or he was sure he was going to win this one.

Over my dead body.

Lennox forced herself to say, "God, I trust You" out loud to make her flesh come under subjection to her faith. She lay on her stomach, positioned her Stryker, and readied her soul to fire. *Keep courage and fight!*

All it would take is one simple pull of the trigger and she could end him right where he stood. Counting down to the shot….

Three. Two. One.

She pulled the trigger and missed Ahab, but got a man to his left. He fell to his knees. When his veins lit up bright blue, he tipped to his side. Men scattered. She quickly aimed again and fired—again, again, and again—so many times, she lost count. As her heart pumped adrenaline throughout her body, she became one with her weapon—fluid and accurate. All the practice at Sparrow City paid off, though she'd have to reload soon or turn the switch to lethal ammo. Regime soldiers fell, one right after the other. Those who remained standing frantically hunted for the one who fired.

Empty.

Her Stryker ran out of bullets. She huffed and pulled her last loaded magazine and snapped it in place.

The enemy was too close. They would be right on top of her in less than two minutes.

She fired, took a breath, and fired again. The men to her left and right shouted at one another and pointed straight to her location.

God, help me! She silently prayed and tried to silence her breathing.

Regime boots stomped her way, slinging up mud with every step. Closer… closer…. The blood-rain fell harder. She blinked the drops from her lashes. Two more yards….

Sky bolted across the valley like a flash of lightning and took out three oncoming men. A second later, he stood in the open, shooting over a dozen more. Each bullet found its target with ease. "Lennox, we have to get out of here. There's too many of them!" he shouted, veins bulging from his neck.

Lennox jumped to her feet, Stryker ready, and steadily marched forward to meet him. To her left, there were more men. She turned and fired. To her right, even more.

No. They had to hold them off for a little bit longer, at least, until more Sparrows arrived. Lennox caught her breath and wondered what had become of Oliver and Easton. Was their side of the bluff overrun with the Regime, too?

Lennox remained steadfast, unwilling to give up, no matter what it looked like. It wasn't about who stood against her, it was about who had already gone before her. She inhaled. Jesus had already overcome every single one of her enemies.

Keep fighting! Lennox demanded of herself.

In her periphery, Sky took down men with his Prowler abilities, controlling the soldiers' minds and then either shooting them or detouring them away from her. But he could not hold that many for long. She rushed to him, but her feet could not push her there fast enough. An exchange of bullets soared through the air. One of the Regime's found Sky's flesh.

He stutter-stepped as he pursued his targets. Lennox grunted and shot every round until there was nothing left. It wasn't enough. She made her way to Sky as more rounds flew their way.

"Lennox, get back!" Sky shoved her. She flew backward and landed on her rear twenty feet behind him. Sky trudged forward, taking on more fire as he controlled men with his mind as best he could in his weakened state.

The whole scene played out in less than thirty seconds, but to Lennox everything happened slowly. She gazed in horror as five men fired at the love of her life. *This can't be happening.* "Sky!" She screamed his name until her lungs were on fire.

As she scrambled toward him, Sky hit the ground like a ragdoll, now a bloody mess upon the earth. His bright green eyes dimmed, fading. Other Prowler men held him in place through mind control. Slaves to Venom themselves, they controlled one of their own.

"No!" Lennox's blood boiled, heating up her entire body. She clicked the switch on her weapon and shot lethal ammunition. She gathered the courage to stand and drew her Sapphire Shield with her free hand. Tears welled up in her eyes and her heart quickened, beating faster as she ran to where Sky's body fell. *No. No. No.* She stood guard over him and held the clear Sparrow tech up to protect them both. "Sky, you're going to be okay."

"You have… to run," Sky managed a whisper.

"I'm not leaving you."

"You have to."

"I won't." She breathed in deeply. "Not again."

Pop! Pop! Pop! Too many Regime bullets flew their way. The sound of the tiny domed killers pounded against her impenetrable shield. Her arm stung from the vibration of the hits as she stared through her clear defense. "This is all my fault," she said under her breath, wanting to rewind the hands of time.

Ahab, the leader of the Regime, approached. His sheer enjoyment at watching the girl who stood fight for her life was written all over his face.

She took aim and fired, hitting Ahab square in the chest. A laugh roared from his belly as tech around him flickered.

What? Only the Sparrows have that type—

She saw Max and Sia in a Regime truck, bound and gagged. Their eyes were wide as they squirmed and tried scooting their way free. Ahab had gained a Sparrow Kev disk.

He threw up a fist and the hail of bullets ceased. "Bravo! Bravo!" He clapped, giving an abbreviated bow toward the bound Sparrow scientists. "Brilliant." He held out his pale hands in front of him, turning his palms up and then down, admiring the protective nanotubes around him. "Utterly brilliant!"

Lennox took advantage of the time Ahab's pride provided and glanced at Sky. "Don't move." She knelt farther down and placed a gentle hand on his chest. "You have to stay here."

Confusion took over Sky's face. "What are you going to…? No."

"Sky, you're hurt too badly." Tears welled up in her eyes as she clung to strength. "Stay still, *please*." Her plan had failed. *Oh, God, what have I done?* Mortars exploded in the distance, catching her attention for a moment. "I have to distract the Regime and you, *you must not move*." Blood poured from his side. "Sparrows will come for you and have you back fighting in no time. You're going to be fine." She held the back of her hand to her nose and sucked in a breath, trying to hold her composure.

"You're lying."

"No, *no* I'm not. You're going to make it and I'm going to make sure of it."

Sky weakly reached out in vain. "You can't do this, Lennox. It's suicide. Ahab will kill you." The love of her life tried to move—to somehow stop her—but his body protested and he winced in pain.

"Sky, it's my turn to protect you." She smiled and bent down to kiss his cheek. "I am not afraid of dying and I won't be afraid of living—of fighting for what I know is right."

Sky's hand gripped her wrist, struggling to hold on, summoning his Prowler strength one more time to keep her safe. "I love you." His eyes faded, his glowing green irises turned dim as his eyelids closed over them. For now, he slipped into unconsciousness. She scavenged for her gauze in her pack and packed his wounds as best she could.

The tears fell as she loosened his grip from around her wrist. "And I love you." As soon as she pried the last finger from her wrist, she stood and held back the sobs she wanted to cry. Even if she wouldn't, he would live to fight another day.

She traced the outline of the *D* on her arm. The scar gave her an undeniable strength like never before. Strength to defy. Again.

She narrowed her gaze on her foes. The time had come to finish this fight. Once and for all.

Chapter 20

The moon and the sun glowed like splotches of blood on a gray canvas. Curious rain still beat down. As Lennox took the first step to her destiny, her feet sank in the reddened mud, leaving footprints to mark her path. She blinked hard and cleared her mind of any distractions. Only one thought consumed her.

Ahab's going to pay for what he's done.

The Prowlers standing close watched and waited like hungry wolves as Lennox walked by, waiting for their Alpha to give the signal. If they wanted to feast upon her fear, they would be sorely disappointed. She had none left. Only *fight* remained.

And fight she would.

"She's mine!" Ahab roared. He matched her stride for stride in the opposite direction, meeting her in the middle of the valley. His expression of sheer pleasure made her want to vomit—being close to him again made her sick all on its own. His sunken eyes gleamed and his hair stuck to his pale skin. He met her gaze with a vicious grin.

Standing feet away from her adversary, Lennox raised her Stryker and fired. Again and again. The bullets bounced off the nanotubes. Tears welled. Nothing she could do would work against him. She felt so small in comparison to what had to be done.

Lennox, lay down your weapons. The still, small voice whispered in her soul. She knew the voice all too well. She had ignored it, quenched it, and questioned it, but here in the middle of battle, no matter how bizarre it sounded and no matter how badly she wanted to say *"But, God,"* she would obey. It was foolish to consider vengeance as her own. It wasn't hers at all, but His.

Lennox deactivated the Sapphire Shield. The clear protection shriveled into itself and formed a rod, which she threw at Ahab's feet.

His head cocked to the right and stared, his mouth agape.

She'd expected him to raise his weapon and fire a bullet into her brain and end it. When he didn't, Lennox lifted the strap of her Stryker over her head and threw that to his slick shoes, too. It stuck in the mud and the red rain clinked against it.

Ahab raised his thin brows. "What are you doing, you crazy, dimwitted girl?"

"Surrendering."

The Regime leader spun around and laughed, arms outright as he looked at his men. "You hear that! The girl who stood is finally surrendering to the man who is king. Now," he said, his snake-like eyes meeting hers and commanding obedience. "She *will* bow."

Lennox squared her shoulders once more, undefeated. "No."

"Excuse me?" Ahab's bewilderment turned to red-faced rage—red like the sun, moon, and rain.

"There's been a misunderstanding, I'm afraid. I'm not surrendering to *you*. I'm surrendering to God Almighty." With narrowed eyes, she pinned him with her stare as the rain dripped from her eyelashes. "May His will be done."

221

"*His* will …" Ahab laughed wryly. "You might as well join me, girl who stood, because you and your so-called God can never defeat me."

Lennox clenched her fists into tight balls, keeping them at her sides. "You're already defeated."

Rage boiled from Ahab's eyes as he approached, spitting his words through gritted teeth. "You want God's will? It would appear His will for you is to die!" He grabbed her chin and squeezed hard. "So tell me, how do you want to die?" he spat close to her ear, his breath fowl in her nostrils.

"With faith." She peered up to the heavens, rain falling upon her face. *I trust Your plan. I trust You.* This was it. She would be a martyr to the cause. Her name would be written with all the others before her.

To live is Christ, to die is gain, she reminded herself, swallowing hard and tightening her fists.

Inhale. Exhale.

Ahab flipped his red-lined suit jacket back and drew a firearm from his leather shoulder holster. He lifted it to Lennox's face until the gun met her forehead.

Fate had found her. She closed her eyes and

waited for the inevitable, envisioning the welcome she would receive in Heaven.

Tomorrow is not promised, but eternity is.

Inhale.

Exhale.

The cold barrel pressed harder against her skin. For a split second, the sound of the trigger being pulled filled her ears.

She opened her eyes.

She still breathed—alive.

In front of her, an irate Ahab released the mag and snapped it back into position. He shook his head and aimed the weapon a second time.

He pulled the trigger, again, again and again. Each time Lennox flinched as it misfired. With bated breath, she waited. Still alive. The Regime leader cursed unrepeatable words, but she remained calm. The sting of fresh tears she would not let fall burned her nose and eyes. With a shouted expletive, Ahab slammed the butt of the gun against her temple.

Lennox fell. She placed her hands in the mud and mustered the courage to rise, wiping the blood from her brow with her palm as she found her balance on her feet. She refused to cower and stared her enemy in the face. Dizzy, but standing, she spoke with her mind made up. "You can knock me down a thousand times and a thousand times I'll rise." She swallowed metallic-tinged saliva and squared her shoulders one last time.

"Is that so?" Ahab shook his head and smirked. "I don't have time for this." He lifted the weapon again and swiftly fired. This time, however, it worked.

Time stretched as the bullet cut the air toward her heart. She closed her eyes in anticipation of the hit, but just as it seemed darkness had won, a brilliant light pierced through the red and gray sky, lighting the forest. Warmth covered her and filled her. She could not see God, but He was here. He was with her, always.

The bullet froze mid-flight.

A loud, triumphant sound unlike anything she'd heard before echoed in the valley of the bluffs—a sound so loud and triumphant that it could not be ignored.

Lennox smiled, lifting her face to the brilliant light shining down from the heavens.

The world quaked. The Regime scattered as a

bolt of lightning traced a fiery line to the ground. Lightning and thunder rolled throughout the valley, but she neither faltered nor feared. The Eastern sky split and the trumpet sounded louder. Great white clouds swirled amongst themselves. Out of the great aperture came the Son of Man in all His splendor, holy and magnificent.

Lennox's body disappeared from Ahab's grasp. His sunken eyes widened and his jaw dropped with astonishment with staggering disbelief.

Lennox gasped. The air tasted sweet. She breathed in again and a pleasant, indescribable aroma infiltrated her nostrils. *Heaven—this is the way to Heaven.* She remembered her dream that seemed so long ago where her parents told her to fight. But this was even better than her dream. It was real.

She watched as everything came together. She held out her hands and marveled at their newness. The dirt was gone from under her nails and scratches no longer lined her skin. Even the air she breathed brought warmth to every part of her, comforting her.

The Defiers and Sparrows were going *home*.

Beyond words.

Lennox's heart swelled with a joy she had never known. She stood, encircled by everyone she loved, everyone she had lost, and every one of them was perfect and whole.

Mom and Dad. Kira. Pop. Clover. Easton. Oliver. Ace. Elise and the boys... *and Sky.* Everyone who believed, present and accounted for. Their blood-stained uniforms and bruised faces were replaced with white robes and healthy, whole bodies.

Far below, but seen with eyes capable of light-year vision, a trembling army bowed in the presence of the Maker of Heaven and Earth. Ahab, himself, crumbled to the dirt, on His knees before the Lord. The man who called himself a king and thought he was god had learned he was neither. No matter how hard he fought to stand, his flesh had no power against the might of God. He remained on the ground, bowing.

Lennox smiled wide at her mom and dad who beamed with the light of joy, and then to Oliver, whose eyes lit up as if he was a small boy.

Finally, Sky. His eyes no longer glowed with

Venom, but with true, immaculate redemption. At last, he was truly free.

Within a twinkling, they were at Heaven's gates made of pearl, standing on a street made of gold as pure as glass and surrounded by walls of jasper so stunning it left Lennox breathless. Nothing she'd imagined could ever compare to this place.

Angels sang, "Holy, holy, holy are You, God!"

One-by-one, Defiers and Sparrows alike, went before the Lord. Just as the stars were written in the sky, so were the names of those who served the Lord written upon His palms. He knew each one by name. He knew their story. He knew their struggle.

As Lennox waited her turn, she thought about everything the Lord had brought her through and saved her from. Why He loved her—why He used her—she had no idea, but she was grateful. Closer and closer she walked toward Him.

In the Heavenly Throne Room, Lennox stepped forward and bowed before her Savior in awe and reverence. She took the crown upon her head and laid it at His feet. Looking up, she smiled at her One True King, no longer hurting and torn. No longer broken.

His mighty outstretched hand wiped the very last tear she would ever cry away and said, "Well done, my good and faithful servant."

No more tears. No more disease. No more hunger. No more war. No more death. After all she had been through, everything she'd seen, everyone she thought she'd lost, she finally had the victory. Her fight on earth had reached its final chapter, but her story in eternity had only begun.

She stood.

She fought.

She conquered.

Romans 8:36-39

"For your sake we face death all day long;
we are considered as sheep to be slaughtered. No, in all
these things we are more than conquerors through him
who loved us. For I am convinced that neither death
nor life, neither angels nor demons, neither the present
nor the future, nor any powers, neither height nor
depth, nor anything else in all creation, will be able to
separate us from the love of God that is in Christ Jesus
our Lord."

A Note from the Author

Thank you so much for going on Lennox's journey with me and for giving the Defier Series a place on your shelves, whether virtual or physical. I know how much time readers invest in books and I am in awe that you would take the time to read all the way to book three! THANK YOU! I am so grateful for you!

A note on the ending …

Okay, so I know that I probably broke a couple of official writing rules and was even warned by my peers that readers might not like it, but this was 'the' ending, even before the first words were written for book one. For me, this is how it had to end.

Caution Ahead, Spoiler Alert

After I saw terrible, real persecution of Christians overseas, I knew Lennox's journey would end in the presence of God, as all of ours will, eventually. Since God placed this story on my heart, I felt it only right to give Him control of how it all worked out and I hope as readers you enjoyed it (if that's the right word to use for reading dystopian novels), even if it wasn't the typical "Happily Ever After" scenario.

I pray you are encouraged and inspired to take a stand for your faith in Christ. As the world grows darker, the people of God must grow stronger to be the light. Even when all hope seems lost, we know that God is able! My dear friends, you are more than a conqueror through Christ who LOVES YOU!

With all of my appreciation and respect,
Mandy Fender

ACKNOWLEDGEMENTS

I never in a million years thought I would write a novel, let alone, a trilogy. Without the grace of God, I would not have finished due to many reasons, but with God all things are possible! He provided peace and strength to complete this crazy dream I had of writing a story about a girl who stood. I hope to be as brave for Him as the characters He impressed upon my heart. Jesus, I love You and thank You for being there for me when I felt like I could not write another word. You saw me at my darkest and yet still loved me through it. Thank You for never letting me go!

To my supportive husband and precious kids, thank you, thank you, thank you. I love you guys more than I can truly express. Brandon, you encouraged me through everything and supported my dreams of becoming an author. Tyler, you kept me laughing with your dimpled smile and crazy, heartwarming antics. Jadyn, you inspired me with your zeal for life and pure, raw determination. All of these things kept me writing and from giving up. I love y'all!

Mom and Dad, you both have supported me since the day I was born. You believed in me when I was just a 'snaggle-toothed' kid and told me I could do whatever I put my mind to and that as long I put Christ first, all things would work out. Thank you for believing in me, always.

Angie Brashear, you, my friend, are a pillar of light in my writing world. Thank you for going through the roughest of my drafts and helping me to make them better. I cannot wait to read your next book!

Laura, Britta, Staci, thank you for working with me and helping me on this path of publishing that I am on. It's a hard, lonely road without friends and peers like you, so I honor you and thank you for your diligence and support!

Serena Chase, thank you for providing an intensive critique from which I learned so much. Your services are invaluable to me!

Elizabeth Miller, you are an editor extraordinaire (totally had to spell check that! Haha!). Thank you for still being willing to work with me even after you have seen the grammatical disaster that is my manuscript. You make my story shine the way I want it to and I am very grateful!

Special thanks to Liv Fisher for allowing me to use one of her tweets as a quote for Lennox. "The beautiful thing is that, even in the darkest of times, there is Jesus. He is light. He is hope." When I read it on twitter on her account, I knew it was something Lennox would say, so I politely stole it. Just kidding, I asked permission. Thanks, Liv!

Huge congrats to Megan Yeager, who won a character giveaway and got to name a Defier in Conqueror. Thank you for entering! I hope you enjoyed reading her story and thank you for the ideas and support! Keep changing the world and fighting for faith!

Church family, I love you guys! Thank you for being so supportive and for not rolling your eyes when I say I have written another book! Y'all bless me!

Beta readers, you guys rock! I appreciate

everything you all do!

Veronica Lynn, we made it! Thank you for helping me survive in my writing world for over three years. Your patience, diligence, and listening ear provided so much strength for this story. Love you, friend!

Finally, many thanks to YOU, the reader, for giving this unknown, little author a chance. I may not have a big name backing me or a huge brand promoting me, but you still jumped in and gave my books an opportunity. For that, I feel like the most blessed writer in the world! If you're reading this, you have helped my dreams come true and I THANK YOU!

Connect

Facebook: Mandy Fender Author Page

Twitter: @mandyfender11

Instagram: Mandy.Fender

Goodreads: Mandy Fender

Website: mandyfender.com

Sign up for Mandy's newsletter on her site for writing updates, book giveaways, and more!

Printed in the USA
CPSIA information can be obtained
at www.ICGtesting.com
LVHW071951170923
758232LV00085B/998